Bang Boy, Die Boy

A Novel

The Movie,
That Became A Book,
That Will Be A Movie.

J. Lewis

iUniverse, Inc.
New York Bloomington

Bang Boy, Die Boy
A Novel

iUniverse books may be ordered through booksellers or by contacting:

iUniverse
1663 Liberty Drive
Bloomington, IN 47403
www.iuniverse.com
1-800-Authors (1-800-288-4677)

ISBN: 978-1-4502-1857-3 (sc)
ISBN: 978-1-4502-1856-6 (ebook)
ISBN: 978-1-4502-1855-9 (hc)

Printed in the United States of America

iUniverse rev. date: 03/02/2010

Contents

Summary

Omega Styles is the star character. He is a drug dealing gang banger that's trying to become legit. His right hand man is holding him down no matter what and he's thinking about becoming legit also. The Feds are on to him; they locked down his father who was a kingpin/ warlord in the game. Omega is doing his thing and he's heading for the same brick wall his father hit. His eyes are starting to open and he's trying to end it before he end up the same way, but as he does, he's hit with dilemma's, struggle, and dyer conflict. As the story goes on you are bedazzled with some of his friends' real life situations and heartaches. "This hood story is several stories in one to make a hood classic". It's a good read, for real people who like real life relating events. All situations are based on true facts, and true events. Follow me as I take you on a journey of **Drugs, woman, money, and murder** and quench your thurst of the real life, streets.

CHAPTER I

"The beginning"

A group of kids walk up to a little girl and her sister. The little girl is drawing boxes on the concrete; the older sister is standing there, playing with her hair. They are talking back and forth. I wanna go first, you went first last time. No I didn't you did. Aunh! Aunh! You did! I don't want to play then. Quietly a little boy walks up and points an enormous 44 magnum at the girls shoulder point blank range and pulls the trigger. **"BOOM"** When the little girl falls, he shoots her again. **"BOOM"** Then he shouts, laugh now bitch! Oh it ain't funny now is it? Is it? The little girl is crying frantically screaming "Daddaa". The little girl's sister screams, "I'm telling my mother" and starts to run, but falls. The other gang of kids' run after her catches her and starts to beat on her, she continues to cry and screams for her life.

Computer Graphics

(Credits roll) A brick wall is being shot at by many weapons. Names are forming creating the credits. Dual 44 magnums pump shotguns, AR-15s, Glock nines, Machine guns, AK 47, all types of Weapons.

4 guys are sitting at a table bagging up drugs. A lady walks in and starts begging for more drugs. 'T please give me another hit the other one didn't burn right. The dealer at the table refuses to give them to her and starts to argue with her. Vick don't start that bullshit, you know my shit is always poppin! You just greedy as all hell. Then he sees her daughter walk in from school, he looks at her like a tiger looks at its prey before the kill, he says to her you don't want no mo a dis. She says yes I do, you got that banger right there. He says well let me get it in with treec. She says that's my baby! I can't do that shit! He says I knew you ain't want it. She looks at him for a minute as he kept running the slick shit on her. So he coherses the mother into letting him have sex with the daughter for more drugs, she agrees. She goes in the room and talks to her daughter, baby! You know mommy is sick right! Well! 'T' has the medicine to make me better, but I don't have no money to pay him, so he wants to spend a little time with you and he'll give it to me free. Treecy says no!!! I don't like him; I don't want to spend no time with that boy. The mother starts crying frantically, treecy I need the medicine bad baby! I can't do right without it please! Help me baby please! The daughter starts crying because she sees that her mother is hurting, she feels sorry for her, and she loves her, so the daughter agrees to the sex. The drug dealer goes in the room and haves his way with the innocent minor.

END OF CHAPTER I

CHAPTER II

"The Crush"

Two girls walking to the corner store, they see Omega and start talking amongst each other, girl! Omega sure is fine and he's nice as hell too, he be lookin out for real though. Ms Brown was having a problem paying her rent because she lost her money and Omega paid her rent for two months. The other girl blurts out 'say word' she says "word" Omega looks over and he recognizes them and calls them over. Yo Mira, Sheeka, come here for a sec and he starts to conversate with them. What's poppin? They say 'nothing, just chillin.' One of the girls likes him, however, she beats around the bush about letting him know it, so she uses another approach. She asks him, 'Mega' when are you going to let me braid your hair? He responds one of these days, I be real busy trying to eat, gotta stay on my grind feel me. Sheeka says 'ah hah' no doubt and they continue to conversate for a while. Then Sheeka says o.k. Time for us to be out, if I leave it up to y'all we'll be here all day and we got somewhere to go. Then the girls say goodbye and walk off to the store. Omega's right hand man says to him, man I don't know why you just don't go ahead and smash that. Omega responds I don't want to have to get into any drama with her fool ass boyfriend K'mar, because I would have to kill him.

"Meanwhile"

"A few minutes later" Monty and his sister Treecy are walking home from school. They are talking amongst each other; 'Treec I got an 'A' on my test today! Treecy says that's good Monty keep up the good work if daddy was here he would take us out to eat and shopping for your good grade. Monty says I know, I miss him, I wish he was here. Treecy says me too Monty, me too. Omega sees them, stops them, and asks how are ya'll doing? And how is your father doing? Then he notices that they are wearing beat down shoes and clothes. Where is all ya'll new clothes at? He is concerned about them and all of the nice clothes they use to have; and why they are dressing the way, they do recently. They explain to him, sometimes we don't have no food in the house, so we sale some of our clothes to our friends to get money to eat. Then they explain to him that some of their clothes end up missing along with other nice things that they have had. So Omega's first thought was that their mother is selling her kids shit off for drugs. Therefore, he digs in his pocket and hands both of them a one hundred-dollar bill each and says 'here go get something to eat and to come back around later on, so I can take ya'll to go get some new gear. They respond with big smiles and say "thanks Mega" and gives him a hug then continue to walk up stairs to their apartment in the projects.

END OF CHAPTER II

CHAPTER III

"Beef Starts"

Omega knocks on Mira's door to holla at her and to get his hair braided. Sheeka lets him in and says Mira is in the shower; you can come in and have a seat. Sheeka yells through the bathroom door, 'Mira Omega is here to see you! She yells back 'o.k.' and finishes her shower and gets dressed. However, she only puts on Vicki Secrets and a robe, smelling good enough to eat. She approaches Omega and says "hey baby it took you long enough to come see me! He is pleased with what he smells and his mind is running wild with what is under the robe that she has on. Then he says with a smile on his face 'if I knew you was doing it like this I would've been! Up here. She gives him a hug to greet him and he asks her can you braid my hair? She says of course, she tells Sheeka to bring her a comb and the hair food grease. She tells Omega here sit on these pillows. She sat a few on the floor by the coach, and he does. He sits between her legs, and she starts to braid his hair. They make small talk, Mira says 'Mega' so how you doing? He says im I-Iight, you know same ol shit, different day trying to get hood rich or die trying. She says word! I feel that and they continue to converse and about half way through braiding his hair, there's a knock on the door. Sheeka goes to the door and looks through the peek hole. She sees that it's K'mar and she panics. She whispers and tells Mira yo! Its K'mar as K'mar shouts through the door; Mira! open the fuckin door, I know you're in there, I seen someone come to the peek hole, so open this fuckin door! Mira shouts out, "I'm coming" and scared out of her mind she scrambles for her clothes. She remembers how K'mar told her not to have any other nigga's up in her apartment, no matter who it is. So she tells Omega 'go sit at the table and act like Sheeka is doing your hair'. Mira opens the door and greets K'mar with a kiss, hey baby! He kisses her back reluctantly; however, he's suspicious about why it took so long to open the door. She says I was in the bedroom and didn't want to disturb Sheeka from doing Omega's hair. He doesn't believe her and starts to scream at her, what is that nigga doing in here? What did I tell you? She says he's just getting his hair braided, he ain't doing nothing! Omega hears the commotion and gets up to explain, yo! Mira and Sheeka grew up with me and we just cool like that. However, K'mar doesn't want to hear it and continues to argue with Mira Therefore, Omega decides that he's leaving and starts to walk out the door. He knows how K'mar get down and he didn't want any drama around his projects to bring heat to himself to slow down his money flow. However, K'mar took it as he was shook. So as he was walking down the stairs, he hears him say, 'I'll push that nigga right now' and he hears him coming. He starts to run down the stairs, because he remembers that he left his ratchet in his car. And as he gets to the front door, he sees K'mar's boys in a van parked out front, next to his C.L. Benz, therefore, he walks by calmly. He remembers that he doesn't have his burner, but he does have a grenade on him. So he takes the pin out and throws it under the van, then he starts to run. The nigga's in the van don't notice what he does. Now K'mar is out of the building shouting to his boys, "get that nigga." Omega shouts to his boys, "ride or die."

selling drugs in front of where they lived. And if you made sells in, around, or in the circumference of the building, you got dealt with right away. Their father big Dixie had a small army called **"DEATH-BEFORE-DISHONOR"** or **D.B.D.** And all of them were loyal to him to the death, because he took very good care of them. He was fair, however, he ruled with an iron fist. He took his family to church every Sunday and always blessed the church with a substantial donation; therefore, the preacher was always pleased to see him. The preacher use to try to talk some sense into him about getting out of the game. "Dixie when you gonna stop sinning and come do the lords work, it's your calling". However, when he started talking like that, Big Dixie use to tell him "Rev I really can't talk about it right now, I have some important business to take of, but we'll talk soon o.k. And rushed off. Big Dixie liked the preacher because he did a lot for the children and the community. And was a messenger of the lord. Dixie believed in God, he just wasn't beat for the enlightening spills the preacher dropped on him. He would get out, when he was ready. He also had money in other things, such as supermarkets, gas stations, and liquor stores; however, he was a silent partner with the owners. He made sure business stayed good and that none of the businesses were ever robbed. He also had ties to a few police officials and several people in city hall including the mayor. Most people didn't know that. He kept all of his business affairs just that, business and silent.

END OF CHAPTER V

CHAPTER VI

"Time to Celebrate
Get your swagg on"

In the club, Omega is celebrating his birthday. He buys out the bar. Music banging, he's kicking it with his homies, saying it's been a good year. Ladies passing by greeting him. One say's hey! Omega this party is what's up. He says back "what's poppin shawty? You know I gotta ball out for my b-day". Niggas and homies salute him. Its new years and Omega's birthday. Omega has a big reputation, so everybody and their momma was at his party. They party hard, then after a certain hour upstairs in **V.I.P.** They have a lock door; male and female revue. Woman on one side of the club, and on the other side men. In addition to that, anything goes threesome's, foursome's fivesome's and then some. Omega looks across the room and spots K'mar. Then he taps J'Gun and say's "What is this fool doing in here" So him and his homies step to K'mar and Omega says to him, "K'mar, I don't want no shit at my party. We are trying to have a good time, so don't fuck it up!" K'mar says, "I ain't fucking up your party homey. I just come to fuck with some of these hoes, pop some cryst and that's it." Omega nods his head, "I-light then, be easy." K'mar responds, "I-Iight then," and spins off. Omega tells his boys, "keep an eye on that fool," they nod. On stage VS. Is spittin & rippin' hot shit. The crowd goes crazy when he's on stage. A lot of people want to wild out from his lyrics; however, they keep their composure. Omega is feeling VS. Style and he says to J-Gun, "I don't know why that nigga just won't go in the studio, lay some shit down and get a deal with a record company." J-Gun replies, "Man that nigga loves the streets too much and he loves that paper. The nigga stay huggin' the block. The only reason he here now is because it's your birthday." Meanwhile, on the other side of the club, two of K'mar's boys try to holla at two girls sitting in a booth; Zee and Carla. K'mar's homie Fury says to Carla, "dig right, me, you, sip on something, ride, go eat, ride, my spot, smash, then you, OUT!" Carla replies, "Excuse you! Nigga please! Act like Michael Jackson and spin off." Fury replies, "What!" Then they get into an argument. Sweets notices the drama and goes to Carla's aid. Him and Fury exchange a few words. Sweets says calmly "Ayo you need to fall back on the bullshit homeboy, this my homie birthday we don't want nothing poppin off tonight. Fury say's "this bitch tryna act all stuck up and shit like she all that, I don't want you anyway bitch". Carla say's I can't tell Then Omega sees the confrontation. He approaches with J-Gun. He calms Sweets down and asks, "What's the problem?" Carla explains to Omega what happened; She say's "this nigga trippin" and at the same time, Clipse whispers something in fury's ear. Then Omega asks Fury, "What's the problem?" Fury replies, "Naw ain't no problem," and as he walks off, he says to Carla, "ya breath stink anyway, I can smell it from here." Carla says, "yeah whatever nigga, you smell your ass. Spin off creep!"

"Later that night"

After the party, couples start to creep off. Some go get something to eat and some creep to the hotel. Omega, Sweets, and J-Gun are in a car talking to Zee, Carla, and Treeba, who are in another car. They are talking about hooking up back at the projects. Omega say's yo! What ya'll bout to do? Zee say's nothing, just go back to the pound and chill, smoke on something that's it. What ya'll bout to do? Omega say's go get something to eat and chill. Carla and Treeba whisper something to Zee. Zee say's well! Why don't ya'll bring us something back and come chill with us at my crib. Omega looks at his homies' they nod their heads yeah, so then they tell the guys what to bring them back to eat from the restaurant. They also tell them to bring back some dutches blunts and they drive off. Omega and his boys go get the food; and they start talking about all the honeys that were at the club tonight. Omega says, man! You saw how ol' girl in the green was eyeing me! I was about to push up on her until she smiled, her fucking teeth looked like a picket fence. I was like oh' hell no, you won't be putting them shits on this dick. Everybody laughed hard as hell.

END OF CHAPTER VI

CHAPTER VII

"WATCH OUT FOR PO-PO"

Narcs rush the block; Officer Steele and Officer Grimes run up on one of Omega's workers. He say's "I aint got nothing" They frisk him anyway like always, but don't find anything. Karma lives on the first floor, so she sees the Narcs frisking him. She knows that the dude is one of Omega's workers and she knows where he keeps his stash. So she runs to it; and takes it in the apartment. The Narcs keep the dude on the wall and they start to check around. They check the garbage cans and all around, but they don't find nothing. The dude just knows they found the stash and that he is going to jail, however, one of the Narcs come back and signals to the other, nothing. One of the Narcs says, "Get your scumbag ass out of here" and they let him go. He is confused and bewildered; he goes to the garbage can and sees that his stash is gone. Now he has to explain to Omega that he lost the stash when the Narcs ran down on him, however, he is afraid to tell him. Karma sees the dude is confused and afraid, but says nothing. She'd rather wait and tell Omega what happened, because she knows with her story will come a reward from Omega for saving his worker and his stash; that he could've lost if the Narcs would have found it.

"Later on that night"

Its late night' everybody is around drinking, smoking blunts, laughing and having fun. Music is blasting and some people are diddy boppin' around. The Narcs roll up deep, nobody runs except one person. He say's "oh shit the Narcs" and tries to run. This dude is so drunk, that he can barely walk, let alone run. One of the Narcs walks along side of him as he tries to run and says, "where you think you going" then snatches him up by the collar and throws him to the ground. The other Narcs harass the crowd of people and frisk them. Several of the dudes talk back and say, "we ain't got nothing, why ya'll always fucking with us" Some they don't check, because they know already that they will never find anything on them. The officer checks the guy that tried to run and he finds a sleeve of dope on him. He say's "jackpot" Omega and everyone else look at the drunk dude like he has five heads or something. They all know that when you're smoking, joking, and drinking on the block, 'shop is closed' you put your work up until later. When you sober up, you punch back in. Dude looks at Omega with a face like, get me out. Omega nods to assure him that he will without even speaking. The Narcs talk slick, "yeah we got one" "time to go to jail buddy" and all the smart ass sarcasm shit they could think of while pushing guys around and jumping back into their cars, one say's "catch you later ass holes" as they were pulling off.

END OF CHAPTER VII

CHAPTER VIII

"SUMMERTIME IN THE HOOD"

It's the weekend; Omega and all his homeboys always have a cookout once or twice a month in the summertime, depending on the weather. They pay for 2 ice cream trucks to stay all day, giving out free ice cream cones. They pay for entertainment. They pay for rides for the children and all kinds of beverages, big barrels of soda, beer, and alcohol. All the food you can eat and take home. They spend at no expense to give back to the community they grew up in and protect. Besides, they make more than enough money from these same people, so it's only right to show love. The children always have so much fun and Omega makes sure that he gets on the Mic to talk to the kids. He tells them "make sure y'all stay in school and get your education, because it was very important. And in order for y'all to survive in the world today you're going to needed it. You'll need it for now and for later, because of the heavy competition that's in store for y'all in the future". The kid's were always so very happy when he had these events that they screamed with a lot of enthusiasm. **"We are going to stay in school and get good grades."** Omega was always pleased to hear that from them at these events. Omega always had one of the hard working ladies of the projects; get a permit to block off the streets, so the kids can run around safely. The Narcs never gave them too much of a problem when they gave these events. However, they weren't too far away; and every now and then, they would show their faces. Officer Steele didn't like Omega too much; however, he respected what he did for the kids. His niece and nephew were growing up in the projects, because he had a good for nothing sister that still lived there, that was strung out on drugs. Plenty of times he tried to get her help, but she would end up right back on the glass dick. Pulling and sucking on it as if she were giving the love of her life brain. The pipe wasn't her first love, however, the speed she was going, it was certainly going to be her last. She use to be one of the prettiest girls around until a tragic event happened in their family that devastated her.

"SOMEWHERE IN THE POUND"

A man and a woman were getting high in the hallway of the building. They're in the back exits getting needles ready to shoot up. They fire the dope up by cooking it up in a spoon, and they use the needles to insert the deadly chemical in their veins. However, before they can inject it, two Narcotics police officers bust the back exit door open and surprise them. Its officer Steele and officer Mendez. Officer Steele smacks the needles on the floor with a large flashlight and starts to scream on them. "What the fuck are y'all doing shooting up in the hallways" They say nothing. They just stand there looking stupid. He tells one of them "you look a fuckin mess; you need to check into a drug rehab". They still say nothing. So he grabs the woman by the arm and takes her down the hallway to talk to her. He says, "I should just lock your ass up, you look like straight shit." She replies, no! Don't lock me up, I'm trying to do right, but it's hard. I don't want to go to jail; I got to take care of my kids. He looks at her and says go your ass in the house and get some rest; and I better not see you out here no more tonight. She agrees by noddin her head and saying o.k. Then he walks off and say's to Officer Mendez, let's go. However, before he leaves he picks up the needles and throws them in the incinerator, then they walk out of the building.

END OF CHAPTER VIII

CHAPTER IX

"Sex me"

Omega is sitting in his 745 convertible, one of his many cars that he owns. As he is talking to Sweets, he hears someone calling him, Mega! Meeda Mega! He looks up and it's Karma, standing there as fine as she wanna be. Karma is one of the baddest Spanish mommies around. She is about 5'5, 130pds, a handful of titties, very perky, not to big, not too small. A big booty, co-co complexion, and curly long hair. Omega's manhood instantly stands at attention. She says to him, "Meeda Papi! I need to talk to you, and it's very important". Omega says, "Karma I can't right now, I'm busy." He knows that if he gets into it with her, he won't get any business done until tomorrow. Karma had a way of getting you into her apartment; and you wouldn't want to leave until the next day. She was very gorgeous, but she fucked for bucks. She says to Omega, "Look papi! It's real important and it will be very beneficial for your pockets". She now has his attention; if there was anything Omega liked more than money, it was new money. He was thinking that Karma had one of her cousins from Columbia; hook him up with a better price on the keys of dope he was getting. So he gets out of the car and she grabs him by the hand and leads him into the building and into her apartment. Inside of Karma's apartment, she had the place laced with all kinds of expensive stuff. A 55 inch flat screen plasma TV, butter soft leather coaches, 10ft long aquarium, and plush rugs on the floor; you had to take your shoes off at the door. Very nice paintings on the walls, and a king-size bed. She had the works in her crib. She tells Omega she'll be right back, she goes in the room, takes off her clothes, leaving on her Vicki secrets panties and matching bra. She then reaches in her drawer and grabs, the bag of drugs she got out of the trash can; the day the Narcs ran down on dude. Then she grabs a box of the many boxes of condoms that she has. She has all kinds, assorted colors and flavors. She calls Omega to the room. Meeda! Mega aqui once he gets to the door, he sees Karma layed across the bed, legs wide open, sitting up on her elbows. On one side of her a brown paper bag and on the other side, the box of condoms. He says "Karma I don't have time right now" She says, look Papi, I'm about business you know that, well this is business. In this brown paper bag are your drugs that I took from the trashcan the day your boy almost got knocked. I swiped it before they searched it, so they let him go. On the other side, you know how I get down, so I took care of you, now you take care of me. Besides I ain't had none of that dick in a minute, you done got stingy with it pa! He laughs and says nah! When you put it on a nigga, you have him in the fetus position with his thumb in his mouth, making baby noises and shit and I got to get this money, I can't get this skrilla if I'm fuckin with you all the time "feel me". She says I'm good at what I do pa, that's why you got to pay, to play. He says, "I heard," She says, now get over here. Omega walks toward the bed; Karma sits up on her knees and starts to take off his shirt. She kisses him all over his chest. Then she unbuttons his paints and belt. She can see his dick bulging out of his boxers. So she stands up and pushes him down on the bed, pulls off the rest of his clothes, and takes off his boots. She stands over him dancing, taking off her

Vicki secrets. She grabs the condom seductively and smoothly, like poetry in motion. She opens the condom and puts it in her mouth while gently stroking on his penis. She slides her warm mouth on his hard dick, placing the condom on at the same time. She sucks for a while, while he plays in her dripping wet vagina. It's so wet that her whole inner thighs looked like water was poured between her legs. She moans softly and so does he. She straddles him and goes to work on him, taking in every inch of his manhood. They fuck like supercharged rabbits for hours. By the time they got finished, it was the next morning. They both were soak and wet in the bed, lying there exhausted. Omega sits up in the bed and calls Sweets on the cell phone, because he knows he done bounced with his car, waiting all them hours. Sweets answers the phone and says, "what's good doggie". I see you got held hostage for a minute. He says, "Yeah man" and they both start to laugh. Sweets says, I'll be there in a minute, let me sneak away from ol' girl I-Iight. Omega says, I-Iight E.S. While Omega was on the phone, Karma had jumped in the shower. Omega goes to the shower and jumps in with her. She starts to kissing and rubbing on him. He says to her, didn't you get enough? She says, "I can never get enough of you pa! You got the magic stick." He laughs, she smiles. He says, no' for real, I got to go. She says, "Alright, alright" cono and finishes her shower, hops out and brings him a clean towel to dry off with. Once out of the shower, Omega puts on his clothes and he hears the car horn blow. He looks out the window and its Sweets with his car. He goes in his pocket and peels off Karma five hundred dollars for her time and another thousand for saving his package. The package was worth about 15 grand, so it was worth it. As he was leaving, he tells Karma "good looking; I'm a send the same dude that almost got busted with it, back to pick it up". She says, o.k. Papi with a smile; and he leaves out the door. He gets out of the building and looks down by the other building and yells out dude! Dude runs to him. He say's to him, Karma got something for you, go get it. Next time put some of that shit up and take the trips up and down the stairs. Dude says, Mega this shit goes so fast, it don't make no sense. I finished the other package already. Omega says, I know, but make the trips. It's better safe, than sorry. Dude says, "I heard" Omega starts to walk off and says; I'll pick that other thing up in a minute. Dude replies I-Iight. When Omega jumped in the car, Sweets starts to look at him smiling saying yeah! Caliente whipped it on you Hah! Omega smiles back and say's maaaann! She fucked the blowers off of me.

END OF CHAPTER IX

CHAPTER X

"He's Free"

It's about 2:00 clock in the afternoon; Zee, Treeba, and Carla are standing in the front of the building 4. They are talking about getting their hair done and coping some new gear etc. A car pulls up while they are talking and gossiping. A dude hops out, Zee and Carla sees him, but Treeba's back is turned. Zee and Carla smile. The dude puts his finger over his mouth to tell them to don't say nothing, they don't. He covers Treeba eyes and disguises his voice and say, what's good shorty? Guess who? Treeba starts cursing him out. "Guess who? Nigga who am I, Woody Woodpecker or somebody. Who the fuck I look like, Ms Cleo, like I'm psychic, like I'm a know who you are with these big ass hands over my eyes." The dude removes his hands and Treeba turns around and screams at the top of her lungs, like someone had just stabbed her in the chest. **"AHHH"** It was her brother Ma'lik; he had just got home from prison. He was taken away from his family when he was 10 to a youth house for 2 years; he also had five years probation. However, he violated probation and ended up doing about 6 years total, then he came home. That same year he went back to prison for aggravated assault and possession of a weapon and got a 6 with an 85%. His sister loves him dearly, they were real tight. She use to send him money and letters all the time. He says "yeah! What's good y'all" and gives Zee and Carla a hug. Treeba is hanging on her brother's arm, she's happy he's home. Omega and J-gun pulls up in a new Cadillac Escalade XL with TVs all up in it, wooded out and a system you can hear before you see the truck coming. They see Ma'lik and say, what's poppin homey? Ma'lik says, me, you, the hood. They say that's what's up. Ma'lik says I see y'all still eaten lovely, still getting that skrilla. Omega says, we got to do us, you feel me. Ma'lik says, right, right. So Omega says, what's good? I know you just getting home and you wanna smash some guts, know what I'm talking bout, but let's take this ride to the mall and get you a few things, feel me. Ma'lik say, that's what's up; and he jumps in the truck. Omega looks at the girls and say, what's up with y'all? They say, nothing, we just chillin. He asks Zee, where your car at? She says, in the back parking lot. He says, come on, let's ride; and bring your girls, my treat. They say allll'right! That's what I'm talking bout baby, Mega be **"BALLIN"** he says let's roll. They jump in Zee's car and follow Omega to the mall.

"The next day"

Two guys are in the back, getting' their work out on. Doing push-ups and pull-ups on the pull-up bar, it's a daily routine for them. Ma'lik walks up, he says, "What's good homeboys?" They say, "You know 'G' mackin, big backin" big sex says, you need to keep your workout on, fall in! He says, "Nah' I'm good." I get my workout on every time I lift that ratchet ya' heard. Big sex replies, "I smell you." Shim-Shawn asks him, When you gonna come and get some of this money? Ma'lik says, Man you know I ain't got no patience for the block, I need mine in abundance, I ain't no hustler, I stick and move, know what I'm talking bout. Shim-Shawn says,

"I heard." Big sex asks him, have you seen Omega yet? He says, Fo' sure, he blessed me. Took me to the mall, threw some doe at me. Shim-Shawn says that's what's up. Look in my jacket right there, ya' heard. That's you right there homey, a coming home present. Then Big Sex digs in his pocket and hands him a brick of skrilla; that's from ya big brah ya' heard, you deserve it, you put in a lot of work in around here feel me! Ma'lik says, thanks for the love homies; and hugs them both. Then says, y'all know where I'm at if you need me I-Iight! They say, no doubt, trills and he spins off

END OF CHAPTER X

right? They both say, Hell yeah! He says, I-Ight, we'll hit the streets and clubs, we'll find this fool, he'll show up somewhere.

"BACK IN THE POUND"

It's the afternoon; Treecy is just getting home from school. Monty didn't go to school today; he said he wasn't feeling well. It's been several months since their strung out mother had them prostituting for her to keep up her habit. Treecy goes in to see about Monty. As soon as she opens the door, she sees Monty on his knees giving some old dude brain. Monty jumps up, because Treecy startled him. She screams, Monty! What are you doing? Monty stands there looking stupid and embarrassed. She pulls him into the bathroom and starts to scream on him. What's wrong with you? Why are you doing this? They start to argue back and forth, then Treecy storms out of the house and bumps into her mother and screams "this is all your fault" then starts to argue with her about them having sex with all these people for drugs; and starts crying hysterically. Then she shouts, "I'm going to tell my father." The mother screams "tell your father, he can't do shit, He's locked up for life". Treecy storms down the stairs. She's on the stairs crying her heart out, because she knows she ain't going to tell her father nothing. Her father would have her mother killed, if he found out about what she was making his kids do for her. Moments later, Omega and J-Gun walk up. They see Treecy crying on the stairs. Omega asks her, Shorty! What's wrong with you? However, she doesn't want to say anything, because J-Gun is there. Omega tells J-Gun to go head up, he'll be there in a minute; and he does. She say's to him, "my mother got me and my brother, trickin' for drugs and we don't like it, we been doing it for a while and I'm tired of it". Omega gets heated and starts to yell. What the fuck Treecy! Why didn't you tell me this shit sooner? Then he starts saying I will kill that bitch! How in the hell is she gonna have her own kids, trickin like that? He pulls out the ratchet and starts to run up the stairs. Treecy yells, No Omega! No, don't kill her. We just don't want to do that no more, that's all. Don't kill my mother please! Omega. Treecy continues to chase him upstairs, they get to the apartment, Omega runs to the bedroom, and busts open the door. Vicki is sitting there getting high. Omega starts screaming, Vicki! Why in the fuck do you have these kids trickin for your strung out ass? 'Hah' I don't give a fuck if you do it, but you ain't having these kids support you're fucked up habit. Vicki doesn't even care about what he's talking about, she is cooking off of the dope, she just shot in her veins. At this time, Treecy is in the room talking with her brother. Therefore, Omega puts his gun to Vicki's face and says' in a low, angry voice bitch I'll push yo ass right now! Act like you don't hear me. Now she sobers up a little and starts to be scarred. She starts to cry and says, no, no. Omega says, Oh! Now you hear me. She shakes her head and say's "yes". He say's "if I hear about you trickin these kids off to anybody else, you can kiss your ass goodbye. She says o.k. And Omega walks out of the bedroom, calls Treecy and Monty, gives them money and says; "I'm taking y'all to the doctor tomorrow morning, so be ready".

"The next morning"

Omega picks up Treecy and Monty early in the morning, and they are ready to go to the doctor. Monty has been complaining about being sick off and on. Omega takes them to his private doctor. They are sitting in the waiting area while Omega talks to the Doctor and says, "Look Doc, give them a full check-up and check for all types of diseases, the whole nine, alright?" The Doctor says, all right. She asks Omega, "Have the children been sexually abused or anything?" He responds I'm not sure; however, I don't want to make big issue out of it with the state people and all. He hands the Doctor some money and the Doctor says, alright. She goes and talks to them and she tells Treecy, "Come with me". She checks her out thoroughly for everything. After awhile, she tells Omega "she is fine, she's just very sexually active for a girl her age". She then checks Monty thoroughly for everything, and she is startled by the results of the tests. She informs Omega that Monty is very sexually active. He has been penetrated in the anal area, he has several venereal diseases; he is HIV positive and he should be admitted to the hospital ASAP. Omega drops his head and says to himself, "God damn you Vickie." Then ask "Doc" can you make the arrangements to have him admitted. She says, "Yes, right away". Omega goes back into the waiting area and talks to them. He tells Monty you have to go to the hospital, because you are very sick. That's why you're stomach is always hurting, and the reason why you be throwing up all the time and got diarrhea bad. Monty says o.k. However, his sister looks very concerned about what is happening to her brother.

END OF CHAPTER XI

CHAPTER XII

"Good Eaten"

In front of the projects, a car pulls up. The person driving asks for 2 bricks of dope, five guys swarm the car. The one that's serving him says, where's your money? He shows the money, so he hands him the drugs. The car pulls off as he counts the doe. Its real money on top, but beat money on the bottom. The car screeches off burning rubber with a lot of strobe lights and emergency lights blaring off. The dealer screams "get that car" Dudes come out of nowhere, throwing bottles, rocks, anything they can find to bomb the car with. Some pull out ratchets and start unloading at the car, hitting it several times; however, the car gets away. Shim- Shawn shouts, 'get your money first, make sure it's there, then give them the product. Remember that homey.' A station wagon pulls up and parks, It's an elderly woman, Miss Betty. She has a lot of grocery bags from shopping. Times have changed a little since Big Dixie got locked up years ago. They still have the building with all the elderly in it, however, some live in any and every building now. The young dudes are still taught to respect their elders, but you have some young reckless dudes that don't listen until a boss comes around and lets them know what's really hood. Miss Betty needs help with her bags, so as she pays the guy that brought her home from the market, a couple of guys hanging out there, help her with her bags to her apartment. She thanks them for the help and tells them to make sure that they come back later and buy some trays from her. Every week Miss Betty cooks up a storm and sales the food, five dollars a tray. She makes fried chicken, fried fish, oxtails, candied yams, potato salad, cabbage, rice, corn on the cob, macaroni and cheese, cornbread, banana pudding, and barbecue turkey wings. You can have any combination for 5 dollars a tray; and she always sale out because she got people coming from all over Paterson. She makes a killin' off of the projects alone. She tells them don't forget, and tell your friends. They say o.k. And they leave

END OF CHAPTER XII

CHAPTER XIII

"Knuckle up fool"

It's a rainy day and there's a big basketball game going on at the collage. Omega is there with most of his crew; they are cheering on the local team to beat the visitors. Omega always place street bets with other guys on some of the teams he likes. Most of the big balla's always bet. They bet on anything, football games, dogfights, car races, motorcycle races, horses, dice, everything. So as they are cheering on the team, they spot K'mar and his boys. Sweets taps Omega, he says, "I see that fool" y'all be on point. They say, FO'sure, no doubt; and they enjoy the rest of the game. As the game ends and people are walking out, one of K'mar's boys start singing some funny shit out loud. "Ride for my niggas, fuck dem other niggas" Omega and his boys ignore him because they don't want no shit to pop off in the local collage. So as they are walking to their cars, Fury yells out, what's up now Sweets? You was running your mouth off in the club, "Let's see what it do now" Sweets smiles and says, "Nuff said punk". K'mar says, "just you and him Sweets, one on one, no heat". Omega says, you got dat. What K'mar doesn't know is that Sweets may look sweet, but looks can be deceiving. Sweets is the truth with his hands. He's been boxing since he was about 10 years old. He's won the golden gloves 7 years in a row and he use to fight semi pro. However, the money didn't come in fast enough for him and he had to take care of his twin boys, so he resorted to the hustle game, so Fury was in for a surprise. Omega, J-gun, Shim-Shawn, and Big Sex, grab their ratchets out of the car just in case K'mar went against his word. They gathered around and Sweets and Fury started to fight. Sweets was smiling the whole time. Fury was shooting 35 to life at him. Sweets went to work on him, hitting him with a combo from the door; Fury was shocked and mad. Fury had work; he just couldn't fuck with Sweets. Sweets hit him up with another combo, Fury gets one punch in, but now he's real mad and his face is real swollen. K'mar shouts out to Fury, "fuck him up nigga" what you doing? He's beating the blowers off your ass. Fury shouts, "Shut up, I got dis nigga" So Sweets, still smiling, hit him with a hurricane of blows that staggers him and he falls. He's bloody as hell and can barely see. Omega says, that's enough Sweets, let's ride out. Sweets puts his hands down and grabs a napkin out of his pocket. Omega says, we out! K'mar couldn't do nothing, but watch as they got into the car and pealed out. Fury still dazed says, fuck dat! And runs to the car and pulls out a Mack 10 and starts shooting like crazy. He hits Omega's car, Omega says, what the fuck? And looks in his rear view mirror and sees Fury running toward him firing off. He steps on the gas to pick up speed. Big sex, J-gun, and Sweets start to fire back. They get into a car chase, firing off at each other like crazy. They blaze back and forth and run a light. The police are sitting at the corner, they see the chase and they start to pursue. K'mar says, chill fool, the cops. Fury calms down and they still try to get away. Omega and Sweets car's had work done to them, so they jump on the highway and take off. They both are street racecar legends, so after awhile they disappear, but K'mar and his boys get caught and go to jail.

END OF CHAPTER XIII

CHAPTER XIV

"LAY EM DOWN"

One day Vita was visiting some of her family in Passaic. She spent most of the day in Passaic. As she starts to leave to come back to Paterson, she stops in her tracks, It's as if she seen a ghost. She sees in a few houses down, the dude that robbed them at the mall. She back tracks and tells her aunt "auntie if you don't mind I'm going to stay the night". Her aunt "says o.k. Baby, whatever you want". Her first plan was to call Omega and the boys and have them come deal with this fool, but that might bring too much heat. So she decides she'll handle it herself. She say's to her aunt I'll be back, I just got to get a few things from the house to wear; and I'll be right back. She jumps in the car and speeds home. In her apartment, she grabs a few things and she grabs the sniper rifle she brought from a dope head, that use to be a Green Beret in the service. She takes her time getting back to Passaic, because she doesn't want to get stopped by the cops. She gets to her aunt's house and she sneaks in the back door. She puts her things up and on her way out of the room, she bumps into her cousin. Her cousin asks her, girl! Do you wanna go out tonight? She says, yeah! We can do that. I just brought some new clothes; I'm dying to put on. She says o.k. We'll leave about

11-11:30 alright. She says, alright. So now Vita has to put her plan together. She sits on the porch thinking it out, saying to herself how am I gonna do this? As she's thinking of her plan, she sees Ol' boy go back in the house up the street. She decides that she's gonna take care of it later on tonight. She sees that the house he keeps going in and out of is a crack house, because several other people keep going in and out as well. So she knows he'll show up soon enough again. A few hours pass; Vita and her cousin start to get dressed for the club. Vita keeps looking out the window to see if the dude will show up again, he doesn't. Her cousin says, "its time to go" however, she procrastinates to leave. They finally leave around 11:45. They get to the club, have a few drinks, and dance awhile. Vita tells her cousin she has to go to the bathroom; her cousin is into her dancing, so she leaves. She sneaks out of the club, jumps in the car, and rides back to the house. She parks a few blocks away from the house. She uses the back door to get into the house. She creeps upstairs and looks in on her aunt; she's fast asleep. She goes in the bedroom and waits by the window, peeking out. After a few minutes, she has luck on her side; the robber shows up and goes in the house. Her heart starts to race from the adrenaline rush. She grabs the sniper rifle and cracks the window. The street has no lights on it, so it's mostly dark. She sets up for the kill. After a minute, the robber walks out; she pulls the trigger. Three hot pieces of death find their target. Two in the head, one in the neck. He drops like a wet bag of cement. She puts the rifle up, creeps out the back door and back to the club. She has no problem getting back in, she tells them at the front door, that she stepped out to have a cigarette, they let her in. When she gets back to her cousin, she's still groovin and says, hey girl! This party is off the chain tonight. She responds, it sure is! And continues to dance with a big smile on her face. '**THE ANGEL OF DEATH STRIKES AGAIN**' claiming yet another soul

END OF CHAPTER XIV

CHAPTER XV

"The Payoff""

Omega and J-gun are parked downtown Paterson by the radio shop, to go cop a couple of CDs. Omega is driving his Austin Martin. Jet-black outside, jet-black inside gut, TVs, loud system, 26-inch Sprewell rims. As he steps out of the car, the Narcs pull up. Its officers Ben Stickler and Meagan Bunzs. Officer Stickler steps to him and says, "What's up scumbag" Step away from the car, you and your boy; they step away. Officer Bunzs is at the rear of the car; hand on her pistol. Officer Stickler starts to check the vehicle and say sarcastic shit like. Boy! You guys must be in the rap business or something, driving around in shit like this. He checks the under the seat, the trunk, the doors, and the glove compartment. He finds what he's looking for, in between the side of the seat and the armrest. He slides the envelope in his jacket. He then signals to Officer Bunzs, nothing. He approaches Omega and J-gun. Look! I don't like y'all; you drive around in these expensive cars and don't have any jobs. I don't know what y'all do, but I know it can't be legal; and tell your homies in the projects, I'm watching them, and shop is closed today. Omega says nothing. He's just standing there smiling, but J-gun is ready to black out, but he doesn't. He just shoots the Officers a 30 to life. The Officers get in their car and drive off. J-gun says, "Them muthafuckas be trippin" Omega says, relax it's nothing. Omega knows the routine; J-gun is in the dark. Omega just paid Stickler off. Stickler told him; 'in so many words' that they are watching the projects hard today; and that they're going to raid. So don't have any of his boys out there working and don't have any work up there today. Omega was taught by the best, Big Dixie. He always told him to keep his business associates and connects silent; and so he does.

END OF CHAPTER XV

CHAPTER XVI

"Street Ball Legends"

Today, there's a street basketball game in the projects. All of the street legends are there including, Shim-Shawn and Big Sex. Big Balla's from all around are there, because they bet on these games. They bet on whose going to dunk next, who's going to make the next three pointers, whose going to make who look stupid. Since they be having the games on street basketball courts, everybody be there to catch the show. Mothers, fathers, kids, everybody. All of the players are showing off. Some of these guys got skills better than the NBA players. 'Damier' is like a Kevin Garnet. 'Just' is like a Michael Jordan to the fifth power. 'Prince' is like an Allen Iverson with modified handling. The best out here today would beat the best five on the US Olympic team any day. Watching these guys out here is like watching a modern day Harlem Globetrotters with all the tricks, alley oops, handle, passing, it's extraordinary. These guys are the best around. Everybody is having a nice time and enjoying themselves.

'Meanwhile'

Several blocks away, K'mar and a few of his comrades are creeping up in a big, blue, excursion. TVs, loud system, 28-inch chrome rims, smoking blunt, pumping Snoop Dogg's 'drop it like it's hot'. They are talking shit about Omega and his comrades. One of K'mar homies Clipse says, "Yo" if this nigga is there I don't want to hear shit, I'm a just start dumpin on this fool". They know about the street games that be going on, so they are hoping that Omega and his homies are there, so they can start some shit. 'Meanwhile' back at the game. Damier, Shim, Just, CL, Y-Kim, and all of the other street legends continue to do their thing. Most of these guys could have been somebody, but they were immersed into the drug game. Whether it be from impatience or family problems. They have no strong support system, so they choose the streets. Some make it out, however, most don't. As the game goes on, a truck continues to creeps up slowly. Tinted windows start to let down, all of a sudden, **BOOM, BOOM, BOOM.** Shots ring out like in Vietnam, aiming for Omega and his homies, but hitting anybody. (Bullets have no name on them) So reckless aiming puts the life of others in danger. Several people get hit. Adults, children, and all. It's a very horrific scene. Omega and his comrades always carry heat, so they start to chase the truck and fire back, hitting the truck several times with the intentions of killing. One of K'mar's boys gets hit. 'Clipse' He says "oh shit, I'm hit son, I'm hit." Damn this shit burns like fuck. Fury says, you I-light! He says, I'm I-light, I can handle it, I got this. However, the bullet finds its way to a fatal organ. Clipse keep saying, I'm good homey, "I got this" "I got this". However, his pulse starts to fail, his eyesight starts to get blurry, his heartbeat slows down, he goes out... Fury yells "Clipse" "Clipse", however he doesn't answer back, he's dead. Back at the basketball court, there's a lot of Mayhem going on, screaming, crying and shouting because several people get hit including three little children. Two die instantly; and one is fighting for her life. 'Shim-Shawn' gets hit in the leg, 'just' gets shot in the arm. Six adults are hit. Three die; and the others are hospitalized. Omega is frustrated, and he thinks to himself that he has to kill K'mar, before K'mar kills him.

END OF CHAPTER XVI

CHAPTER XVII

"Secret Assassin"

Mira and Sheeka are up in the club drinking and talking. Zee, Carla, Vita, and Treeba are there too. Omega is in the V.I.P. buying out the bar, hollering at some chicks, his usual. Treeba and Vita approach Mira and Sheeka. Treeba is yelling at Mira, bitch! You almost got Mega pushed and I don't like that shit. Mira responds, bitch! That wasn't my fault. He wanted his hair done, I wasn't fucking him. Treeba says, whatever bitch! You wanted too; and you know your fool ass boyfriend ain't got no sense what so ever, and you just keep pushing up on him. Mira screams, so what bitch! Don't hate. What! You mad at me, because he don't want your stank ass. Treeba yells BITCH!! I don't want him, that's my big brah; and I will whoop your ass for him, that's right. Mira yells back, BITCH! You won't do shit to me. A whole big commotion breaks out, Vita and Sheeka are screaming, so a few bouncers break it up and separates them. Vita says, "Girl let's get away from these stank ass bitches" so they start to walk away. Mira shouts out "y'all better leave before ya'll get dat ass kicked" Vita stops in her tracks and shoots Mira a 30 to life, then continues walking. 'Sometime later' when everything calms down, Mira and Sheeka were sitting in the V.I.P.booth. They're both saucy from the alcohol. Sheeka was just running off at the mouth, but Mira is

Quite, she ain't saying nothing. Sheeka is still running off at the mouth, Mira is still saying nothing. Sheeka looks up at Mira; she's slumped in her seat. Sheeka says, this bitch done fell asleep. But then she looks closer and she sees two bullet holes and blood leaking from Mira's chest, she starts to scream frantically. A few people around her see Mira and they start to scream. Then the people start to run for the door. The music stops. Bodyguards surround the booth where Sheeka and Mira are. The D.J. is telling everybody to stay calm. Security locks the door. After a while, the police enter the building. They start to search everyone in the club, however, the assassin is far gone by this time; and no one knows what happened.

"A Few days later"

Officers Meagan Bunzs and Devon Steele, see Treeba,

Vita and Zee standing out front of the projects by building 4. They park and approach them and officer Bunzs says, "You two have to come with us, you're wanted downtown for question". Zee says, for what? We ain't doing nothing. They are escorted to the car. Zee says, what is this all about? Officer Bunzs says, you'll find out when you get there. When they get downtown, they are placed in two separate rooms. They are questioned about Mira's killing. The police were told that, Treeba and Vita were the one's arguing with her in the club. A homicide police officer comes in and asks Treeba, so tell me about the argument. What was it over? She says well! I cursed Mira out, because she almost had my brother killed.

We was just arguing back and forth, but nothing happened, because security separated us; and then we left the club, because we didn't want any drama. And after that we went home. Another

CHAPTER XIX

"TAKIN CARE OF B.I."

Omega and J-Gun go to see Karma in her apartment. Omega needs her to drive for him. He wants to conduct some business out of town. When he walks in, he gives her a hug, and J-Gun says, what's good Caliente? Karma says, Como esta papa. Omega says, Karma we come here on business. She says, DAMN PAPA! I didn't know you like ménage trios, I'm wit it but it's going to cost you. He smiles and says, you are a straight freak, but that's not what I want. I need you to drive a car to Washington for me. It's going to be loaded, but I'll pay you five grand and put you up in a hotel. She says, you know I don't like that type of business, but since I like you papa, I'll do it. And one more thing, he says, what? If anything happens, you pay for a good lawyer. He says no problem. Karma says o.k. When do we leave? He says, tonight around 12 or 1. I'll let you know, so be ready. She says o.k. Papi. Omega and J-Gun start to leave; Omega reaches in his pocket, hands her $3000 dollars and says, you'll get the rest when we get back; then they walk out the door. J-Gun smiles at Karma and says, see you later Caliente! She says, smiling, Oh' get out of here boy; and punches him in the arm. Karma closes the door and counts the money. Then she goes to put it up in a safe that she has hidden in the closet. Later on that night, Omega knocks on the door. Karma runs to the door and opens it. She sees that it's Omega and says, I'm coming, let me grab my things and lock up. He says, o.k. and he tells her, don't worry about your place, my boys are gonna keep an eye on it for you. She says I-Iight! And she locks her door. They walk outside and he say's to her, jump in the ford explorer that's parked in front of the building. There's a phone in the armrest, but don't use it to call me. I'll call you when its time to talk; and use the earpiece, so you don't get stopped. She says o.k. and they ride out. She follows Omega all the way to Washington, staying a safe distance away. When they get there, he meets up with his boys, Tic and Rob. They are from up north, but they have been getting money in Washington for years. They meet in a secluded area and they take the truck that Karma was driving. She jumps in the truck with Omega and J-Gun and they take off to get checked into a hotel. Once at the hotel, Omega goes to get the rooms. He say's 3 rooms please, but Karma say's to him 2 rooms. I'm a stay in the room with you papi, unless you got other plans. He smiles and says 2 rooms please. They check in the Embassy Suites. Omega didn't have to show his face, all he had to do was get the product there; Tic and Rob did the rest. Omega brought down 10 keys of pure heroin. He brought them from Karma's cousin for 60 thousand a key; and sold them to Tic and Rob for $110 thousand a key. Then Tic and Rob re-sold them for $150 thousand a piece. It was pure uncut, so you could make 2 keys off of 1, if you knew how to cut it right. You had to be a true chemist to do so; and still, you would get an 8 and a half or a 9 of good quality dope. On Omega's trip, he would be taking home over 1.1 million dollars for three days work; and Tic and Rob would be clearing over 2 million, so they were very happy. Omega didn't do business with them often as they wanted him too, but when he did, they were always pleased with their profit. Because when he brought it, he brought it heavy. That night, they brought Omega back 900 grand; and told him that he'll have the rest by tomorrow. Tic and Rob had parts of Washington on smash; and they had other dudes from down south coping off them, bringing hella money; so it came fast, and in abundance. That night, Omega, J-Gun and Karma, went to IHOP's.(International House Of Pancakes) to eat. IHOP's had a lot of fine waitresses working there. One in particular was eyeing J-Gun. She was a caramel complexion, around 5ft 11inches, medium build, she kind of favored Tyra Banks, pretty eyes and all. She kept flirting with J-Gun with her eyes, and smiling. J-Gun was doing the same. A waitress approaches the table and asks, may I have your orders please. Before Omega and Karma can say anything, J-Gun says, excuse me sweetheart, I don't mean no disrespect, but can you please have the tall waitress come over here and take our order; then hands her a fifty dollar bill. She smiles and says, this isn't her table, but I think I can handle that for you. She then walks over to the waitress and whispers something in her ear. She smiles and starts toward the table. She smiles and says, hi I'm precious, may I take your order please. Omega and Karma order, than she looks at J-Gun and says smiling, how about you sir, what will you be having? J-Gun says with a big smile, what do you recommend lovely? She says, I tell you what, let me do you, I mean, place it for you and I guarantee; you won't be disappointed. He says, is that right! She says, oh' without a doubt; smiling. He says, alright then. And she says seductively, I'll be back with your orders shortly. Anything to drink while you wait? Yes a picture of orange juice and a couple of sodas. She says, I'll be right back; and winks at J-Gun. Soon as she walks off, Karma says, iye papi! Someone wants a big tip and I ain't just talking about money; and she smiles. Omega says, dawg, she want it. Go ahead and snatch her up real quick, know what I'm talking bout. He says, yeah! I'm there already. She comes back with the drinks and says, here are your drinks; and hands all of them napkins, but on J-Gun's napkin was a phone number. He smiles at her and asks, how long before you get off? She says, about another hour. He says, do you have plans after that? She says, not really, me and my girl was going to hang out, but she'll understand if I have something else to do. He says, that's whats up. Would you like to catch a movie or something? She says, sure! He says, we'll stay here until you get off. Later' after they ate their meal, it was almost time for precious to get off work. She asks them, are y'all alright? Do ya'll need anything else? They say no; and she hands them the bill. J-Gun grabs it and digs in his pocket and peels off a few hundred faces; and says, keep the change. She smiles and says, thank you. She walks off and comes back after a few minutes and says, I'm off, but I have to go home and change. J-Gun says, how about this? We go to your spot, pick up what you need, and you can change over by me. She says, o.k. sounds good. He says, let's roll. Omega and Karma walk out in front of them, they jump in the truck. J-Gun and precious stop for a minute she says, my car is over there. She has a 2007 Mazda 929. He say's to Omega I'll see you back at the hotel. He says I-Iight and he pulls off. They ride to Precious's apartment. She says you can come in if you want; he obliges. Once in her apartment, she gets a few things, She say, so where you from J? He says, Jersey, but I'm here visiting a few friends. She say, ooh' A jersey boy hunh! He says, yeah, born and raised. She says, I can tell you're from up north somewhere, because ya'll dress a little different up there. He says, is that right! She says, yup! That's right. Then she comes out of the bedroom with a mark cross duffle bag and says, I'm ready. So they leave the apartment and jump in the car. While in the car he says, so you live alone? She says, yeah, but my girlfriends come over from time to time to keep me company. I've only been here a few years, I'm originally from L.A. I was going to collage here and when I graduated I decided to stay. He says, what did you go to school for? She says pre med. I'm going back to finish to become a Doctor. I just had to take a semester off to catch up on my bills. The job at IHOPS is just part-time; I work full-time at the hospital. J-Gun say, damn ma! You work hard for your guap hunh? She says hell yeah! I got to, ain't nobody gonna take care of me, but me. He says, right, right. She says, wait a minute! We doing all of this talking, where am I going? He says, oh' I'm sorry, I'm at the Embassy Suites off the highway. She says, I heard that place is nice. I always wanted to go there. He says, what stopped you? She says, I ain't had nobody to take me. He says, now you do. She says, really! He say, really, true story. She says, I hear you, but what about your wife or girlfriend back in jersey? He says, I ain't gonna lie. I have friends I see from time to time, but nobody serious. She looks at him squinting her eyes and says, "J" you lying to me just to get what you want? He says, I wouldn't do that. I try to be honest from the door, because lies lead to more lies. And besides I might forget what I lied about, so it's better telling the truth, because the truth, you never forget. She looked at him like she wanted to rip his clothes off right there in the car, but she kept her cool. However, in between her womanhood, she was moist from his seductive honesty. They arrive at the hotel, took the elevator upstairs and stopped at Omega's room. He seen a do not disturb sign on the door, but yet he still knocked. He heard moaning and groaning and then a loud "go away." It was Karma yelling it out, because her and Omega was in there putting in work. They knew it was him knocking. He yells, I'm next door. Karma yells with a moan, "mmh hmm o.k." He looks at Precious and starts to laugh, she laughs softly too, then they go into the Suite next door. Precious sees the room and says, this is nice! A Jacuzzi, a lot of space, big screen TV. This is the spot. She points to the bathroom and tells him, I'm gonna take a shower and change if you don't mind. He says, of course I don't mind, we can still catch the last movie. She says o.k. I'll be ready in a minute. He says, I'll be right here. She smiles and walks into the bathroom. J-Gun goes over to the bar, pours himself a drink and sits on the coach. He watches a movie that's on cable. He can hear the shower turn on and his mind wanders to the bathroom. He's imagining her taking off her clothes and stepping into the shower soaping up, cleaning herself slowly. Soaping up her breast and stomach, then going lower to her soft, bushy, love box. He imagines her wiping it slowly and repeatedly. After a while of his imagination running wild and him sitting there with his eyes closed, she creeps up behind him and covers his eyes. He places his hands over hers and says, you smell good. She says to him, I was thinking in the shower, instead of going to a movie, why don't we stay here and make our own. He smiles at her and say, whatever you want ma-ma. She say, open your eyes. She releases his eyes and when he turned around to see her, she had on some red thong underwear with the garder belt and a red string strap bra too match. Some red pump slippers and her hair was wet and curly. She had flawless skin. No stretch marks, wrinkles, or blemishes. Her whole body had looked like if she had just gotten a tan on the beach. She was even more gorgeous than he had imagined. He had got an instant boner. She looked down at his large dagger and smiled. She says, I take it that you're pleased, because we have company. He smiles and starts to kiss and caress her. She says, "J" I don't do this often, matter of fact, I haven't had sex in about 2 years, so please be gentle o.k. He says, I got you baby. I won't be rough unless you tell me too. She starts to strip him of his clothes slowly. He continues to kiss her and nibble on her neck and chest. She shivers as he nibbles. He strips her of her Vicki Secrets she has on. She starts to moan as he kisses her between her thighs. Her legs start to shake uncontrollably. She starts to suck on his fingers and chest. She kisses his stomach and scratches him gently. Hard enough for him to feel it, but soft enough not to leave a scratch mark. J- Gun picks her up and carries her to the bedroom. He lays her on the oversized, king-size bed. He continues to kiss her slowly, then he turns her, on her stomach; and massages her neck. She moans and says, that feels so good! I haven't had a good massage in a while. So he continues to massage her back. She says, look in my bag, I got some baby oil in there. He gets up and looks in the bag and gets the baby oil. He then looks in the drawer and grabs the condoms he has. He then pours the baby oil on her back and start to massage her shoulders, arms, back, ass, and legs. She is in sheer ecstasy. He then turns her on her back, and looks her in her eyes. She is feeling what is happening to her. He massages her breast, her stomach and legs. He pours some baby oil in between her legs, she moans passionately. Then he rubs on her love box. She continues to shake and shiver. He begins to gyrate her clit and she start to make all kinds of provocative noises, "aah, mmh," J-Gun's magic stick starts to rise again. He is ready to jump on her, but he doesn't. Since its been a while for her, he wants to make sure she is very pleased and satisfied with her first episode with him. He continues to rub on her love box gently. Then he puts his head in between her legs and buries his tongue in the love box. She climax instantly. He continues to go to work on her. She climax again, and again, orgasm, after orgasm. She orgasms very hard and long. You can tell by the way she throws her head back and screams with pleasure; and by the way she tries to pull J-Gun's head deeper into her. J-Gun is now throbbing with pleasure. So she pushes him back and grabs a condom and gently slides it on his love dagger and starts to go to work on it. Massaging, licking, and humming on the nuts. J-Gun is pleased. You can tell by the way he moans. "After a while" he orgasms and starts to breath heavy, however Precious is not finished. She lets him calm down a little, then she starts kissing on his waist and stomach again to get him excited once more. He begins to feel it. His magic wand starts to rise. Precious grabs the baby oil, rubs some on him, places a condom on him, then she hops on him. She is on top, but backwards. His face is in ecstasy. She rides him like a jockey rides a horse. Up and down, side to side, teasing him by going to the tip, then taking it all in. She starts to moan wildly and says, "I'm bout to cum, I'm bout to cum." He say, "give it to me baby, let it go." They are breathing heavy; and sweating like Hebrew slaves, working on a pyramid in Egypt. He begins to orgasm. They both are about to explode into sexual bliss. They both yell with joy, then fall to the bed in each other's arms. J-Gun takes a deep breath, and Precious exhales.

END OF CHAPTER XIX

CHAPTER XX

"AMERICAN GANGSTA"

In the prison, Big Dixie is well known and well respected. There are a lot of organizations and affiliates in the prison system. Bloods, Crips, Latin-Kings, N.E.A.T.A.S., Muslims, God Bodies, Arian Nation, and Disciples. You name it, there, there. However, Big Dixie is older and wiser; and they all respect him. He is known as one of the best that ever did it. When the F.B.I. ran down on him they took his Mansion, his cars, jewelry, and over 100 million dollars he had hidden in a floor safe in the Mansion. Over 20 million dollars he had in drugs, at all the spots he had in Paterson and in jersey period. The penthouse he had in the Alabama housing projects, they found over 5 hundred thousand in cash, and 650 thousand in heroin, along with an arsenal hidden in a secret wall. Most of the time Big Dixie was working out with the other old heads that stayed in shape. One day while he was working out, a young dude he knew from the projects was brought in, (a new arrival) the young dude was there on a white collar crime. He liked forging checks and embezzling from big corporations. This dude was the truth, he was a professional if you ever seen one. The young buck did his thing, coming off with several hundred thousand of dollars at a time. Big Dixie had respect for him, because he was getting money, but not from drugs. He sees Big Dixie and gives him a big smile and greets him with a hug. Dixie says, what's up young buck? He says nothing B.D. They got me again, this time I got a 4 with a 2. (Whenever young buck gets caught, he never does no more than 2 to 3 years, because of the white collar crimes) Dixie asks; buck what's going on in the world? He says, same o'l shit, different faces. How are my babies doing out there? Are they going to school and all? Young buck looks at him strange and says, yeah, they still in school, but. Big Dixie says, but what? Spit it out. He looks at Big Dixie and says, is there somewhere else I can holla at you in private? Big Dixie says, hold up. He puts his shirt on and says, 'come on'. They walk to his cell and buck says, B.D. I don't want you to get mad at me, but this is the word on the street. Vicki has your children having sex for drugs. She not feeding them right, and she's strung out big time. Big Dixie gets a look on his face that can kill; he has blood in his eyes. He can murder somebody right now, namely Vicki. Buck say's to him that the money he left Vicki ran out a couple of years ago. Omega be looking out for the kids. He buys them mad clothes and he makes sure food is in the house for them. He also takes them to the movies every now and then. That puts a little smile back on Dixie's face, but he's still very angry. He says to young Buck, I always did like that dude. I treated him like my own. In Big Dixie's mind, he can remember dealing with Omega's mother before he was even born. He asks young Buck, can you get in touch with Omega? He says, no doubt! When I call wifey, I'll tell her to call him on the 3 way, then you can speak to him. He says,

No; just tell him to give me an address, so I can send him a kite. Young Buck says, fo'sure, I'll holla at him tonight and have that for you first thing tomorrow. Big Dixie gives him some dap with a hug and says, good looking. Then tells him, if you need anything, holla at me. Buck says, I'm good. You know I always got something stashed for rainy days such as this. Dixie say, I hear you, you learned a little something, hunh? Buck says, I learned from watching the best... **you**.

END OF CHAPTER XX

CHAPTER XXI

'TAKIN CARE OF B.I." cont...

Back at the Embassy Suites in Washington, Omega wakes up from a ring of the cell phone; Karma is lying next to him naked. He answers the phone, hello? It's Rob. He says, what's up player? Omega say, what's good Rob? Rob says everything. I need you to come thru here; I need to show you something. Omega say, I-Iight, I'll be there in a minute, let me take a shower and throw on some clothes. Rob says, I-Iight then, "ONE." He knocks on the adjoining door to his suite. J-Gun comes to the door and say, what's good. Omega say's yo! We got to go over by Tic and Rob for a minute. He say, I-Iight, I'll be ready in a minute. J-Gun goes to the bedroom and looks at Precious laying in the bed smiling. She says, good morning! He says, good morning sexy. I have to go take care of something real quick, if you want, you can order some breakfast. She says, no, I have to go to work at the hospital. I have to be there by 9:00, but I'll call you later on. Then she jumps up and gets in the shower. J-Gun had already took his shower; and was getting ready to leave with Omega. In the other room, Omega is finished showering. He say's to Karma, "be ready when I get back, so we can take a ride to the mall for a few things" you can order breakfast. She says o.k. papi. Back in the room next door, Precious finishes her shower and is fully dressed. She hugs J-Gun and gives him a big kiss; and say, I don't have to work at IHOPS today, so I'll call you when I get home from the hospital. He says, make sure you do. She says, I will. She gives him another kiss and starts to walk out the door. When she opens it, Omega was standing there. She says, hi! He says, hi! I'm Omega. She says, I'm Precious; and they shake hands softly. He says, yeah! I remember your name, it's hard to forget. She smiles and says, we'll nice seeing you again bye; and walks off. Omega watches her leave, then he turns to J-Gun and says, she seems nice. J-Gun says, she is, in more ways than one. Omega claps his hands together and says, you ready to ride? He says, no doubt; putting his ratchet in his waist. They leave the hotel and ride out to where Tic and Rob are.

Omega and J-Gun pull into paradise projects, they see Tic and Rob. He points to let them know to park by his car, they do. They get out the car and start to talk to them. Tic says, what's good players? They both say, what's good. Rob says, the rest of that doc is in the car. Omega say I-light! That's what's up. Rob says, the reason I told ya'll to come thru is, because I wanted to show ya'll the operation with the hopes that we could do more business. This whole project is ours. Me and Tic move everything up here; and we have people transporting up and down the coast, but our base is in these projects. Our investment is always protected and secured, if you know what I mean. Omega says, I got you. He asks, how often do you have to take a lost? Rob say, once or twice every 8 to 10 months. Omega says, that's good. What's the pay off? Rob says 50 grand a month. Sometimes a little more, but it's nothing. Me and Tic decided we wanted to bring you in, because your product is better than all the others we have dealt with. We always get a great response from our people when we have your work. And if you decide you want in, we'll triple the count you brought with you.

We'll also make arrangements for a drop off, and pick up, in Jersey somewhere. Unless sometimes you want to come down on some vacation shit, feel me. Sometimes we get the stick up boys trying to come thru, but they get handled. We got some straight killa's up in here with us. Omega says, "I heard" I might have to borrow one of them to handle something for me. Rob says, let me know, I'll send him up, I-Iight, Omega say, cool. Then he says, I always did good business with ya'll, so you know what, go ahead and make your arrangements; and when I get up top I'm a try to get a better price on them thangs, so you can get a better price, I-Iight. Rob and Tic say, that's what's up. Rob says, what are ya'll getting into today? Omega say, nothing much. We're gonna hit the mall, maybe a club later. Rob says, come to our spot later on tonight. We got a club called "Whales" its where all the big boys hang out at. We'll show you how we party down here, "ya heard." Omega say, I-Iight, that's what I'm talking about. They all hug and say they'll get up later. Rob says; snatch the bags out of the trunk; as Omega and J-Gun walk off. Omega says, gotcha, and nods his head. They open the trunk of Rob's car, grab the two duffle bags in there; and put them in the back seat of the truck, and drive off. Omega says, check the bags. J-Gun opens them. They are full of money. One has a Mack 10 in it and a note that says "for protection." He shows Omega the note. Omega says, this might be the start of a beautiful friendship. But we still have to be on point and feel them out, to make sure we can trust them.

"AFTER AWHILE"

Omega and J-Gun get back to the hotel. They use the card key and go upstairs the back way, once upstairs J-Gun takes the bags and brings them to his room. Omega opens the door to his room and Karma walks up to him with a burgundy thong on, burgundy pumps and a red rose in her mouth. Her titty nipples are like baby pacifiers, hard and perky. She has a tattoo that starts above her belly button and ends below; it says, "Ridiculously Slippery, when wet." She has the bed covered in rose pedals and a soft cinnamon candle burning. She gets close to his face and says, hey papi; I've been waiting on you to come back all morning. He looks at her in a trance, he doesn't know what it is about her, but he always gets an instant boner when she comes on to him. She grabs his hands and gives him a seductive kiss, he kisses her back, then he says, you are trying to wear me out mamma. She says I told you I can never get enough of you; you give me white liver papa. He says, don't you want to go to the mall? I thought women loved to go shopping. She says, we do, some of us just love a big thick dick first, then shopping. Then she smiles. He says o.k. Let me call J and tell him to give us a minute. She nods and starts to strip him as he's on the phone. He tells J-Gun, yo dawg; I'll knock when I'm ready. J-Gun starts to laugh, I-Iight homey I'll count the doe, he says I-Iight E.S. Karma has him ass naked and goes to work on him. She starts to brain him. He says, by the time we leave here, I'm going to be owing you half of what I made this weekend. She says, papi sit back and enjoy the ride, because this weekend is on me. She works her magic on him enjoying it just as much as he is.

"A LIL LATER"

In the truck on the way to the Galleria mall, Omega asks J-Gun, everything good with that guap? He says, yeah, so far, the first bag is good, but I didn't finish the other two. Omega says, I-Ight, we'll finish when we get back. Did you tip the housekeeper, and tell her to skip the Suites? He says, Yeah. When they arrived at the mall, Karma says, WOW! This shit is mucho Gigante. J-Gun says, English! Caliente, speakee de English! She smiles and says, I'm sorry, this shit is very big. Then she says, I know they got to have a Lord & Taylor here; and a Niemann & Marcus. They look on the mall map. She says, Mega, can we go here? He says, yeah, we need to hit an Armani spot too, if they have one here. Karma says, they got one; and they have a Ferragamo here too, we definitely need to hit that. Then she says, damn! They got all the hot shit here. They even got Issach Mizrahi. He says, let's roll then. They go to Lord & Taylor first. Karma picks up some things while Omega and J-Gun watch. She asks them, "Does this look nice"? They both shake their heads simultaneously, like trained puppies. J-Gun gets a ring on his cell phone. It's his new friend 'Precious.' She says, hey! Boo-boo. He says, what's up presh? She say, you done made up a nick name for me already hunh, that's a good sign. He asks, what size do you wear? If you don't mind me asking. She says, I don't mind. I wear a size 5, why? He says, I have a surprise for you. She says, yeah! I like surprises. She says, am I going to see you later? He says, no doubt. She says, o.k. call me whenever you're ready, I'll be home in about 3 hours. He says, alright, I'll see you later; and they hang up. J-Gun says to Karma, Caliente! Can you pick something out nice for me size 5. She says sure hun, what do you like to wear. The clothes or the lingerie. He responds, it's not for me. She says, I know, I'm just playing with you block head. It's for your new friend. He shakes his head yeah. I'll pick her out something real sexy just for you o.k. papi. He says, yes please, I'd appreciate it. She picks up a few more things. She says to J-Gun, you like her? He says, yeah, I do. She's cool and she's smart. She's in collage to become a Doctor; and she works at the hospital too. Karma says, besides IHOPS? He says, yeah. Karma says, O'l girl is trying to do her thing hunh, I ain't mad at her, we gots to eat the best way we know how. Karma lays the clothes on the counter. The young lady at the register rings them up, and says, that's 11 hundred dollars even. She starts to go in her wallet, but Omega stops her and says I got it; this spree is on me, so get whatever you want. She smiles and says, that's what I'm talking bout papa; and gives him a kiss. They leave the store and go to ferragamo. Omega and J-Gun pick up a few things. Karma helps them by picking things out saying, ooh papi; this will look real sexy on you. Dressing them both on the sneak. They stop in a shoe store and pick up shoes. Karma picks up some manolo boots and shoes. She's having a ball, because she's getting whatever she wants, and she's not spending her own money. A bunch of chicks walk in the store, they are dimed out. They start to eye Omega, J-Gun, and Karma. Karma notices it. She says to them, ya'll have some admirers. They say, yeah right! She says, true story. Those girls have been eyeing us since they walked up in here. I'm a woman, believe me, I know. Want me to hook ya'll up? J-Gun say, "nah" I'm good. I'm hooking up with Precious again later. Before Omega could say anything, Karma says, "oops too late" here comes one of them. Tall, dark chocolate, young lady steps to them and says, excuse me, but would ya'll like to come to a party tonight? And hands them a flyer. Karma takes the flyer and says, yeah! We would like that. The young lady says, my name is mocha. I'll be there tonight hosting the party. It's at Whales, off of central. She gives Omega the eye and say, I'll look forward to seeing you. It starts around 11pm o.k. Karma says, I-Iight, we'll be there. Omega says, I'll definitely be there. Then says, to J-Gun, aint that Tic and Rob's spot? He says, yeah, I think that's the name he said. She says, oh' ya'll know Tic and Rob? Omega says, yeah! Their friends of ours. She says, o.k. well definitely make it then, the club is off the chain o.k. I have to go before my girls leave me, hopefully I'll see ya'll tonight o.k. bye; and winks at Omega before leaving. Karma looks at Omega and says, she's on you papi, for real. If I wasn't here, she probably would have been all over you. But I guess she wasn't sure who I was with, you, or J-Gun. J-Gun and Omega laugh. Omega says, you got all of this from just saying hi! And inviting us to the club? Karma says, yeah! You don't know! You better asks somebody. I know all of the signs papi. Omega says, I see that. Then he pays for their stuff; and leave the store. J-Gun says, let's get something to eat, I'm hungry. Omega says, I could eat something too. Karma looks at him and grins. He says food Karma, food. She removes the grin off of her face. They go to the food court and eat. As they are sitting at the table eating, another set of girls are eyeing them from afar. Karma says, ya'll have more admirers, ya'll are just celebrities down here. Ya'll shining with the platinum watches and chains. I guess if I didn't know ya'll, and seen ya'll in another town; I'd try to holla too. J-Gun says, do you have telepathy or something, because it seems like you know what every girl around here is thinking. Karma says, I'm a woman, I know these things, because I do it. J-Gun says, we hear you Caliente. Then the girls' waved. One signals Karma to come over there. She points to herself, and says me? The girl shakes her head, yeah. Karma gets up to go see what she wants; and as she does, she says, to J-Gun and Omega. Let me find out they on some freaky shit and want me; and smiles as she walks off to their table. Once at the table, they all say hi. Then one says, hi girl! We don't mean to bother you, but we want to know, which one is your man? Because we trying to holla at the one that's not. Karma says to her, neither one. They are my homies, we are just cool, so ya'll can holla if ya'll want. They all give up their numbers; and say, ooh girl' tell them to call us for real, because they are fine! Karma laughs and says, ain't they though. Then one says, ya'll need to come to the club tonight. Karma says, don't tell me girl, "Whales". She says hell yeah! They be off the chain and all the balla's be there too. Karma says, we heard. We will be there, trust me. They say, o.k. Karma says, o.k. then. They say, nice meeting you; and make sure they call. Karma says, I got you. Then says goodbye, and walks back to her table smiling. Then says, look what I got; and hands them the phone numbers with names on them. J-Gun says, "Damn!" These girls down here don't play, do they? Karma says, they know a good thing when they see it. Omega says, ya'll ready to go? They both say, yeah. Then Karma says, one more stop papi please! I got to get something. He says, alright. They go to the smell good store. She picks up some Issey Myaki, Georgio Armani, Sean Jean, and Dolce

& Gabana. Omega starts to reach in his pocket to pay. She says papi! Let me get this one; and hands him and J-Gun a bag each, and say, this is my gift to ya'll. Then she paid for the products, and they left the mall.

END OF CHAPTER XXI

CHAPTER XXII

"TAKIN CARE OF B.I." cont....

Omega, Karma, and J-Gun, get back to the hotel. They get up to the Suites and Omega say's to J-Gun, I'll be over in a minute, just let me put these bags up real quick. When Omega layed the bags down, he sees the red-light on the phone blinking. He says, Karma! Can you please check the messages for me? I'm going next door to help 'J'. He knocks on the adjoining door. J-Gun opens it and says, I turned the machines on already. He says, cool. Then he sits a duffle bag on the table that J-Gun grabs from under the bed. He starts to place stacks of money in the machines. They have five machines in all that count ten thousand dollars at a time. By the time they were finished, it was over 1 million dollars; and an hour, later. He calculated the money they had spent at the mall, so the count was good. They packed the money away. When they were finishing up, Karma knocks on the door and says, Rob called. He said what time are you coming to the club? And do you need him to meet you to show you the way there? He says, I'll call him back and get directions. Its 7:00pm now, so we still got a little time. We'll roll out about 11. Omega asks J-Gun, yo' you gonna asks Precious to come? He says. I'll call her and see what's up, but I don't think I want her to know what's good yet, feel me! I feel you homey. J-Gun says, she might be a keeper. Omega says, if she's a good girl, that's what's up. And at that precise moment, J-Gun's phone rings. He looks at the number on the phone and says, speak of the devil. Omega says I'm a cool out for a minute; all that running around in the mall got me beat. J-Gun says, I'll be ready, when you're ready. Just holla at me. Omega says I-Iight! Then closes the adjoining door. J-Gun answers the phone, hello? Precious say, what's up? He say, you. I was just about to call you. She says, really! He says, yeah. We just got back from the mall and I got something for you. You gonna come get it, or you want me to bring it over? She says, I'll come over. I ain't doing nothing, but sitting here watching TV. And gossiping on the phone with my girl. Give me a few, and I'll be on my way. He says o.k. She says, did you eat yet? You want me to bring you something? He say, I'll wait till you get here and we can order in. She says o.k. I'm coming, bye; He say bye, and they hang up. J-Gun jumps in the shower and relaxes until Precious arrived. About twenty minutes later, the phone rings. The clerk at the desk says, Ms Precious is here to see you sir. He says, let her up please, thank you. A few minutes later, there's a knock on the door. He walks to the door and opens it. There stands Precious looking sexy, seductive, sensual and sultry. She says, hey! Boo-boo; and kisses him soft on the lips. She walks in and takes off the long, Burberry trench she has on. Under that, she has on stretch pants and a t-shirt, smelling like Vicky Secrets apricot lotion and body splash. J-Gun smells the erotic aroma and his blood starts to boil. However, he doesn't want to get into anything with her just yet, because they have to go to the club. So he fights the lovely sight and the smell that's affecting his penis like Viagra. Precious sits on the coach and says, I've been thinking of you all day, today. My co-workers kept looking at me saying, girl you are in a good mood today. You're smiling, and your face is glowing. You must a had a goodnight last night. And all I could do was smile. He looks at her and says, was it that good? She say, ooh my god, what! I told you I haven't had sex in a few years, I wasn't lying. So I had a lot of built up stress and frustration I had to release. I was sooo' tense, but you made all of that disappear for me last night. Now you got me chasing, like you introduced me to some type of new drug I can't get enough of, but that's a good thing. J- Gun says, stop trying to sup me up; then he blushes like a teenage boy. Then he says, what are we gonna order? She says, lets order some sea food, I love seafood. He says what! Me too. Lobster, shrimps, clams. She says whatever you like. He says o.k. Then he looks in the food menu, picks up the phone and starts to order all kinds of stuff off of the menu. He asks her, what you want to drink. She says, a few coolers would be nice, or some Zinfandels; apple flavor. He asks the man over the phone, do you have Champagne and Zinfandels? The man says, yes we do sir. He says, o.k. bring me a bottle of both, that's it. The voice over the phone says, it will be ready momentarily. J-Gun says, thank you. Then he starts to tell him the room. The voice says, we have your room number already sir, so your set. J-Gun says o.k. great! Thank you; and hangs up. Then he turns to Precious and says, we going to a club called Whales, would you like to go? Precious responds, unh, unh, nooo, I don't play the clubs like that. I don't like guys grabbing all on me and stuff, those days are over for me. Besides, I have to go to church early tomorrow. J-Gun says, "Hmm" a god ferring girl "hunh." Precious say, yes sir, born and raised in the church. J-Gun says, that's what's up. Then he says, so you're leaving me tonight? She says I can stay if you want me too; I just have to go get a few things from the house. He says, I would love for you to stay, so do that. By the time you get back, the food should be here. She says o.k. and puts on her coat and walks out the door. J-Gun picks up the phone and dials Omega's room and says, Mega! You up? He says, yeah, were Just watching TV. Coolin. J-Gun says, come to the door. He says, I-Iight, and hang up. A few seconds later, Omega knocks on

says how are you baby girl? She says, I'm fine; I came to see if you'll dance with me. Omega says, I don't dance, but let's go. She grabs his hand and leads him to the floor, they start to dance. She say, is Karma your girlfriend? He says, no' she's a business associate. She says, o.k. what's up with me and you? You busy after this? He say, nah' I'm just going back to the hotel. She says, can I come? He says, sure! But Karma will be there, we are in the same room. She says, I thought she was business? Omega smiles; she is. She says, ooooh' well if she don't mind, I sure won't mind. Omega says, she won't. Mocha says, well I'll see you when you're ready to leave. He says fo'sure. Then they continued to dance for a second, then she hugs him and say's, I got to get back to work. He says o.k. and they walk off. Omega goes back to the table. Rob say, had a good dance player? Omega grins and shakes his head yeah. He then leans over and whispers to Karma. "Were gonna have company tonight" She leans back over and whispers, as long as she doesn't try to fuck me! We alright, and she smiles at him. Another girl from earlier approaches. She's very attractive, light skinned, hazel eyes, shoulder length hair, about 5ft, 8inch, and thick like Trina "The rap artist" She says, hi to everybody, then she looks at J-Gun and says, can you dance with me? He says, I tell you what, let me buy you a drink. Tic says, drinks are on us, just tip the waitress. J-Gun says, I-light then, and invites the young lady to have a seat. J- Gun says, what's your name? She says, Kenna, but my friends call me Ke-Ke. He says, my name is J-Gun. My friends call me J-Gun; and he smiles. She says, o.k. then; and grins. He asks, who are you here with? She says a few of my girlfriends. We come here every so often to have a good time. This is the best spot around. He says, where your man at? I don't want to get you in trouble. She says, I have no man. If I did, I would be in his arms somewhere, not here talking to you baby. I know how to keep a man happy; they just keep going to jail on me. J-Gun says, I'm sorry to hear that. She say, when I deal with someone, I'm loyal to them. But I tell them, if you get locked up I'm out! At least I be honest. A lot of woman don't do that, they just do them when he leaves. Or they string him along like they are being loyal, when they are really sexing his friends and all, so I be straight up from the jump. Enough about me. What about you. Who are you J-Gun? J-Gun says, ain't too much to tell! I'm a young, black businessman, and Entrepreneur. Just trying to take care of myself, and own something's I can leave to my kids. She says, so you have children? He says, no' but I do want some. I just haven't found the right one yet, but I'm working on it. She says, really! He says, really. She says, I want to have some too someday! Maybe in a few more years, when I'm like 25 or 26. He says, how old are you now? She says, I'm 23. He says, 'hmm.' She says why, how old do I look? He say, nah' you look your age. She says, oh' o.k. with a funny stare, good answer; then she smiles. She say, so where is your girlfriend or wife? He says, I don't have a wife. But I do have friends I see, but no one serious yet. She says no commitments? He says no commitments. We can be friends right! She says, of course! Here, take my number again, just in case you lost it the first time. And she digs in her purse, grabs a pen, and writes it down. She places it in his shirt pocket. She asks, where are you going after this? He says, back to the hotel. I'm meeting with someone I just met. She says, oh' o.k. if it doesn't work out, call me, and maybe we can get together. He says, no doubt! I'm leaving tomorrow, but maybe when I come down here again, we can get up. She says o.k. I would like that. O.k. let me get back to my girls, but I want you to call me 'J.' He says, I will; and gives her a hug and say, you be easy shorty o.k. I'm a send ya'll something to drink over there. She say, o.k. thank you 'J.' Then she waves bye to the rest of the people sitting at the table. They say, bye back to her. On stage, Mocha announces a female dancer named "Cream." The guys start going crazy over her, throwing money, and not ones. Five dollar bills are the lowest they tip the girls with here. There are no singles in "Whales" its policy. So all the big balla's have knots of fives and better. They make it rain up in there, that's why it's called Whales. "Only big boys can play in deep waters." J-Gun calls the waitress over and tells her to take table five, 2 bottles of armendale. Then peels off a couple of franky faces. Then he walks to the bathroom and calls Precious. She answers, Hello? In a low seductive voice. He says, you sound so sexy over the phone. She says; stop it, you making me blush. I'm just checking to make sure you're alright. She says, I'm fine! I'm just watching a movie, and talking to my girl on the cell phone, waiting on you to come and put me to sleep. He says, we are leaving in about another hour. The club is hot though! She says, really! You having a good time? He says, yeah! But I will have a even better time when I get there with you. She says, don't I know it, I'll be waiting. He says, alright, I'll be there in a minute, let me get back. She says, alright! Bye. When he got back out of the bathroom, there was a male dancer 'Nestly' up on stage. All woman and a few suspect men, surrounded the stage. He keeps it moving and went back to the V.I.P. booth. He doesn't see Karma, so he says where Caliente run off too? Omega points with a laugh. She is at the front of the stage, dancing, smiling, and throwing money, having a good time. J-Gun laughs and says, that girl is crazy! Omega says, I know, that's why I'm big on her. The dancer 'Nestly' was making the woman go crazy. They were in a uproar, like they were at a Jay-Z concert or something. 'Nestly' finishes his set, and all of the girls don't want him to leave, but its time for another dancer's set. It's another female dancer by the name of 'Juicy.' So all of the men start to crowd the stage again. Karma gets back to the table. She's out of breath, and happy. She says, adios mio! That guy is off the chain! Tic says, I'm glad you're having a good time. She says, am I! This club got it going on, true story. Omega says, you almost ready to go? She says, No! But I'll leave anyway. You can stay if you want. Tic or Rob will get you back to the hotel safely. She says nah papi' I'm leaving with you. He says you sure? She says, yup' I'm positive. O.k. let's have one more drink with Tic and Rob. They pour the

Champagne and Omega says, to good business. They all say, "To good business". Mocha sees that they are getting ready to spin off, so she gathers her things and tells one of the girls, that she have to take over. Omega approaches her and say, I'm leaving. She says, let me finish up, and I'll meet you outside o.k. He nods. Rob and Tic walk with them to the truck. They stand by the truck, conversating a little about the club, and how nice of a time they had. A car pulls up, it's Kenna. She calls J-Gun to the car and steps out to talk to him. Outside of the club is live too. People standing around conversing, blasting their systems, drinking etc. Mocha approaches. She's happy and excited. She hugs Rob and punches Tic in the arm with a smile. She says to Rob, I put the count in the safe. He says, o.k. cool. Then she says, and "T" is on the register. He nods. Tic says to omega, get her home safe o.k.! He nods and says, no doubt! All of a sudden, they hear gun fire up the street by the restaurant. Mocha says, 'uup' Time to go! Everyone starts to roll out. Omega holla's at J-Gun, you ready homey? He nods yeah. He hugs Ke-Ke and they say good-bye. They jump in the truck, and Tic and Rob roll back into the club.

END OF CHAPTER XXIV

CHAPTER XXV

"4,5,6, Murda"

Back in Jersey, 2 dudes that hustle together from the projects, go to a big dice game in the city; after a party at the rink in Bergenfield. The dice game always pop off at the Rucker in N.Y. All of the big gamblers be there. Thousands and thousands of dollars exchange hands constantly. 1 minute you'll be winning, the next minute, your losing. A lot of people leave that spot broke; and only a few leave big winners. The 2 dudes from Jersey had lady luck on their side that night. Even the brothers with deep pockets were having a problem with them and the dice. That night, no matter how many times they changed the bones 'dice' The 2 dudes from Jersey were Ce-loing, hitting triples, and head cracking on the dice. Even the big sharks knew when to quit. They had a few games going on, but the one with the guys from Jersey was the biggest one that night. The bank went up to more than 100 grand. They were nervous, but excited. You had guys betting with them and against them on the sidelines. Every time somebody tried to stop the bank, they would head pop; and the crowd would go crazy, like Lebron James got wind under his feet and dunked. The 2 dudes start to say, last bet, last bet, so put the money on the wood to make the bet go good. A few guys place their last bets with them. When the dice was rolled, they head pop, triple 6s. The crowd goes crazy!!! One guy says, un-fucking- believable!!! The 2 dudes total count that they had won that night was 140 grand. They were strapped, so they weren't too worried about getting robbed. They jumped in their car and headed back to Jersey. They were overwhelmed with the money that they had just won. One says, yeah!! Nigga!! We broke them muthafuckas. The other says, yeah!! Son!! We came off. We got a lot of fucking guap in this bag ya' heard, they couldn't fuck with us tonight. They both were happy as hell. However, in the mind of one, he was concocting a plan. He seen the money and he seen opportunity. So he says, I'm a pull over real quick, I got too take a piss. The passenger says, we're on 80 nigga! The driver says, I know, I know. But I got to go bad as hell! It's going to be real quick. He pulls over and runs to the bushes. He takes a second, then runs back. The passenger doesn't notice the gloves he puts on; and he doesn't notice the 40 cal that creeps up on his side of the window. **"BOOM!! BOOM!! BOOM!!"** It's a doney. The passenger dies instantly. The driver hit himself in the head a couple of times and say's shit! Shit! Then he thinks quick. He jumps back into the car, stops by the river, gets rid of the evidence then rushes to the hospital. He jumps out and acts hysterical. He runs to the window and says, help me! My boy is shot! Somebody tried to Rob us and they shot my boy! The medics rush to the car, grab out the passenger, puts him on a gurney and start checking for a pulse. They find none. The driver is acting a fool, crying and all. They try to calm him down, but they can't. The police arrive. They ask him what happened. They take a statement and tell him, he has to come downtown tomorrow to fill out a report. They impound his car as evidence; and tell him he'll have to find a way home. He says o.k. whatever! He catches a cab. And on his way home he is relieved, he pulled it off. With a back pack full of money on his back; and "**The Angel of Death"** smile on his face.

END OF CHAPTER XXV

CHAPTER XXVI

"TAKIN CARE OF B.I." cont...

Back in Washington D.C.' Omega, Karma, J-Gun, and Mocha arrive at the Embassy Suites. They jump on the elevator and head upstairs, talking about the club, laughing and giggling. They get to their floor and as Omega opens the door, J-Gun says, ya'll be easy with my boy! And smiles. Karma says, we are going to put a hurting' on your boy papa. He hasn't got a chance in hell. Mocha says, oh' we'll take reeeal! Good care of him. He might not be able to walk tomorrow, but he'll be fine. He'll have a big smile on his face, trust me! If you hear some screaming, it won't be us, "it's your boy!!!" J-Gun starts laughing real hard. Karma and Mocha pull him into the suite. Omega says, with a grin, "Help me!" And the door closes. J-Gun opens the door to his suite slowly. He sees Precious laying there, sleeping peacefully. So he takes his clothes off quietly and lays next to her, hugging her. She jumps up smiling and says, "you didn't think I was gonna fall asleep on you, did you!!" He says, whoa! Laughing. I thought you were knocked out! She says, please! I've been fienin' for you all day. I heard ya'll coming in the hallway and I jumped in the bed and played sleep; to sike' you out. It sounded like it was two girls with ya'll, but I'm a mind my business. Now' let's get to business. Then she jumps on him. He says, look at you! But naked and ready to go! She says, yup' I don't get it too often, so I'm a get all I can now, because when you leave! I'm going cold turkey again. He says, really!! She says, really!! He says, we'll I'm a see why I can't make it down here more often; or maybe you can come to Jersey sometimes. She says, I would love to visit you in Jersey, now that I know somebody up there. He says, good, because I want you to meet my sister. She says, I hope she likes me. Now! Enough talking. I need you to tire my ass out! And put me to sleep. They start to caress and kiss. They do each other in; and fall asleep in heaven.

"THE NEXT MORNING"

J-Gun was awaken with a kiss. Precious says, hey sleepy head! I got to get ready to go; I have to make it to church. I ordered breakfast for you; and I had a lovely time last night. He gets up and heads for the bathroom. He says, we're leaving today. She says, I know, don't remind me. He says, am I gonna see you before I leave? She says, that's up to you. I'll be home after church, call me. I'll be home about 2:00 clock. He says o.k. I don't think we're leaving until tonight, so I'll call. J-Gun finishes up, brushing his teeth and turns on the shower. She comes in the bathroom and hugs him around the neck and says, I don't know what made us bump into each other, but I'm very glad that I met you, 'Mr. Jaffar Gunthorpe.' He says, so am I 'Ms Precious Gemms' and they kiss passionately. The room phone rings. J-Gun picks it up, Hello? Its Omega. He says, what's good dawg? You alright over there? Precious throws him a kiss and say goodbye; in a soft voice. He winks back at her. On the phone Omega says, hell! No! Man! These 2 vixens wore my ass out, they wasn't playing. They put the blowers on me. Karma trying to outdo Mocha, Mocha trying to outdo her, it was unbelievable! We went from the shower, to the living room, from the living room, to the bed. Dawg!!! We fucked all over this Suite. J-Gun says, where's mocha now? He says, she left about a half hour ago; and Karma is still in bed knocked out! Omega says, is Precious still there? He says, Nah' she just left. Omega says I-Iight then, let me jump in the shower and I'll be over there, J-Gun say's I-Iight! E.S. They hang up the phone. He walks to the adjoining door and opens it. The other suite door is open already. Karma walks pass, ass naked and yawning. She say, good morning papa. J-Gun's eyes get big; and he says, Daaamn!!! Caliente put some clothes on before you make a nigga want to fuck again. She smiles and says, shut up boy! I'm getting in the shower. I aint got shit you ain't never seen before; my shit is just a little bit thicker or smaller. Then she opens the door to the bathroom and Omega walks out. She says, hey papi! He smiles back and say's hey. J-Gun Just shakes his head as if chills went down his spine. Him and Omega, walk into his suite. He says, to J-Gun. Were gonna take another ride by Tic and Rob. They want to show us this other spot their trying to lock down. They say, there's a bunch of wild boys that hustle out there, so its gonna take them some time to take it over. They said the dudes are real reckless, But it's a lot of guap rollin out there. They got a few buyers up there already; and they got the best product now, so it shouldn't be a problem. J-Gun says, I-Iight, you ready now? He says, yeah, o.k. let's roll. Let me tell Karma we are leaving. Omega goes to the bathroom door in the next suite and opens the door. Karma is sitting in the Jacuzzi tub that can fit four adults, soaking, with her hair wrapped up. Omega says to her; we're leaving. We'll be back in a couple of hour's o.k.! She says o.k. papi. What time are we going home? He says, later tonight. She says, can we go to a movie or something? I don't want to be stuck in this hotel all day. He says, yeah. Be ready by the time we get back, we'll do something. She says, thank you papa! Omega say, I-Iight, we'll be back in a minute; and closes the bathroom door. Then him and J-Gun walk out the front door.

END OF CHAPTER XXVI

CHAPTER XXVII

"TAKIN CARE OF B.I." cont...

Omega and J-Gun meet up with Tic and Rob at burger king. They sit in the restaurant and eat breakfast. Rob says, when we leave, follow us and we'll go to the other spot. Omega nods. They finish up their meals and jump in the trucks. They ride for a while and pull up on a long strip called 'the Boulevard.' It's always live out there. Always something popping' off. However, the money flow is constant. They all step out of the trucks. Tic say's to Omega, if we were to lock this block down, we could clear a couple of hundred a night easy! But all the dealers are independent. There's about 15 to 20 crews on this block. We got a few of them buying from us already; we just got to lock down the rest. These boys over here don't mind murdering a nigga either. They put that murder game down heavy! That's why we are taking our time, easing in, getting cool with everybody. You attract more bees with honey, than with vinegar, you feel me playboy! Omega says, I feel you. We'll I'm a make sure you keep the good shit, so you can flood the block, block, with all dat! "Ya' heard." Tic says that's what we want to hear. Rob says, y'all riding out tonight right! Omega says, yeah, Later on though. Rob says, what we gonna do is finish off what we got, hit y'all on the horn in a few days; and send a car up. We'll hit y'all up a day before, and when my peoples get there, she'll hit you up too. She an older, sophisticated, professional looking, white woman. I don't think she'll have a problem traveling loaded. Omega says o.k. On the way back, I'll have some homies follow her to make sure she I-light. Tic and Rob say, cool. Then they see a bunch of dudes running and shooting at each other. They start ducking, but J-Gun is on point. He keeps his hands on his burner. They jump in the trucks and get out of the line of fire. They pull over a couple of blocks up. Rob says, see how shit pop off out of nowhere! We have to take hold of that block, put some order out there to keep the heat off of it. Omega says I might have a way for you to do that the next time I come down; I'm a let you know what's up I-light! Rob says, I-light playboy, I'm open for suggestions. Everything else is good right? Omega says, Fo'sho. Rob says I-light then, y'all have a safe trip back; and we'll holla in a few days I-light! Omega says I-light. J-Gun says, y'all be easy. They say, no doubt! 'One' and they drive off. They make their way back to the hotel. Omega call's Karma on the cell. You ready? She says, Yeah. He says, alright, we'll be there in a minute. Lock up, and meet us down stairs. She says, o.k. J-Gun calls precious. You had a good time in church? She says, always. He say, O.k. get dressed, were gonna go out to eat. She says, o.k. Give me a few minutes. He asks her for directions to her apartment and they swing by and pick her up. When she gets into the truck, she kisses J-Gun and says, hi Omega! How are you today? He says, fine, and yourself? She says, I'm fine. I'm kinda sad, because my boo is leaving me today, but I'll manage. J-Gun says, we gonna be alright Prec. She says, o.k. Baby, I believe you; I just hate to see you leave. J-Gun says, Once I get home I'll call you; and we'll make arrangements for you to come visit. She says, that's what I'm talking bout! They get to the Embassy Suites and Karma is waiting out-front. They pull up. Karma jumps in the truck. She says, hey Precious! Que,

Basa, mommy? Precious says, nada mommy, just chillin'. Karma says, where we going? Omega says, out to eat somewhere! Precious what's a good spot? She says, it's a few around here, but the best one is the soul food spot. They food be off the chain! They're off of Beverly place. Omega says, tell me how to get there. After a while, they get to the restaurant. The valet parks the truck. They walk in. The place is very elegant. Chandeliers, portraits of black art, pictures of famous celebrities, exotic fish tanks, marble floors, and tables, it's laced out. Omega says, table for four please! The host says, right this way please. They get to a table and sit. The host says someone will be with you momentarily. Karma says, this is niiice! Then a waitress comes to the table and says, hi! My name is Kera; I'll be your waitress tonight. Are y'all ready to order or do you need a few minutes? Omega say's no! We ready now, so they look over the menus, then place their orders. What would you like to drink? They order their drinks. Karma says, WOW! Look at the big screen TVs; and no that ain't playing the hova videos. The waitress says, I'll be back shortly with y'all drinks. Precious asks Karma, so you had a nice time this weekend? She says hell! Yeah! I had mad fun. But its time to get back home, I miss my little spot in Jersey. When you come visit, I'm sure 'J' will let me show you around. We can go shopping in New York and hit a club or something. Precious says, I-Iight girl, let's do that. The waitress comes back. Here are your drinks, and your food is on its way. If you need anything else, just asks for me o.k. Omega says, thank you. A few minutes later, the server brings the food to the table. They eat and conversate for a while. They have a good time; and tip the waitress heavy. Then they head back to the hotel to leave. Precious helps J-Gun pack his things. She say's I hope you don't get home and forget about me. He stops packing and walks over to her; I can never forget about you! I just met you this weekend, but it feels like I've known you for years. She kisses him on the lips and gives him a big hug. Omega knocks on the door. You ready? He says, Yeah! Omega opens the door and says, carry this; we have too many to carry. He takes the bag. Precious says; double-check everything to make sure you don't leave anything. He does; and say, I got everything, let's roll. They go down stairs and check out. The man at the desk hands them some security money back. Omega says, give me an envelope please! He does. Omega asks him, what is the young woman's name that took care of our room this weekend? The host says, Maria. Omega hands him a fifty, then puts the rest in the envelope with Maria's name on it. Make sure that she gets this o.k. I'm a call back and check, so make sure. The host says it would be my pleasure sir. Omega says, o.k. Thank you. The manager says, come back anytime; we will be happy to have you. They wave and say, good-bye. Outside, they pack the truck. Karma is driving with the guap. Precious thought it was kind of weird to be driving 2 trucks, but she said nothing. They drop her off and they head back to Jersey

END OF CHAPTER XXVII

CHAPTER XXVIII

"BACK IN THE HOOD"

Omega and J-Gun pull up in the Cadi truck. Shim and Sweets greet him, what's good homeboy! Whats' goody my dude's! Sweets asks how was your trip. Omega says, lovely, lovely. We made some new friends and conducted some good business. What about y'all, everything straight? Shim says, no doubt! Shit went fast though. We got bored, so we hit a couple of clubs and shit that's it. Omega says we'll next time around; it'll be enough for y'all to stay busy. Sweets says, next time. You must be planning to go again soon! Omega says, we'll! We plugged into something good, so it's going to be more often than before. Sweets say's that's what's up. Shim say, we seen that fool K'mar at the game by Putnam oval. But nothing popped off, because it was too many pigs around. They were swarming' the spot today. J-Gun says we need to just push that fool. Once, and for all. I'll do it. Omega say's no 'J' it'll bring heat. I got a plan for that mark. Vita, Zee, and Treeba walk up. They say, hey big brah! And give everybody a hug. Omega says, Tre' were your brother at? She says, I don't know. Somewhere robbing or up in somebody's ass. 'They all laugh' He says, yo' tell him to holla at me when you see him, I-Iight. She says I-Iight. He say, where y'all going? Vita says to get our hair and nails done, where else. He says, here, it's on me. Treeba says, see! That's why you my dude, true story; and gives him a hug. The girls start to walk off to Zee's car. Omega say, don't forget to tell him to holla. She says I got you big brah. Then he leans on the hood of the truck and says to Shim, Sweets, and J-Gun. I'm thinking about bringing Rob and Tic in. How y'all feel about that? J-Gun says, their cool, their on point, so it's I-Iight with me. Shim says, the couple of times I've met them, they seem like they know what's up; and they ain't on no bullshit, so, its I-Iight with me. Sweets say, they my dudes. I was feeling the way they move when we first met em, so it's cool with me. Omega says, see this is the thing. They got shit poppin off down there, but it's a spot that has no order, no structure. Niggas just be on some wild boy shit. So if we bring them in, let them know what's good, give them some structure, they could get them dudes on point down there; feel me! Sweets say that's what's up. Omega say, o.k. What I'm gonna do is have them come up; and were gonna let them know what's good. I got to get in touch with Sha' cause I need him to do a few things. Put him on the payroll real quick ya' heard! Shim says, he's by the laundry; I'll run and get' em. At that exact moment, Omega's cell phone rings. Its Young Buck. He says, what's good Mega! He says what's really hood Buck. Young Buck say, you nigga, me, and the block, ya' heard! Omega says, I smell you nigga. Buck says, listen. I'm locked down right, wifey is on the 3 way; feel me. Omega says, right! Buck says, I ran into B.D. and he needs you to holla at you bout something serious, ya' heard! Omega says, right. So he wants you to hit me with some info, so that he can holla at you a.s.a.p. Omega says, I-Iight then. Tell him to hit me at 40 Pearl St, 07511; and I'll get it, and hit him back. Buck says that's what's up. Omega says, tell that nigga I said what's up and to keep his head up. And if he need me, holla anytime and he's good I-Ight. Buck says, I heard. Omega says, you good Buck? He says,

I'm always good homey, you know how I do. So you'll see me soon, feel me! Omega says, I heard. Buck says, tell them niggas I said stay up; and be easy ya' heard! And you be easy; and be safe homeboy. Omega says I-Iight! E.S. Then Sha' and Shim-Shawn walk up. Sha' says, what's good my dude! Omega say, what's good lil'Brah; And they hug. Omega says I want to put you on something. I know if shit pop off, you can outrun mutha fuckas. I need you to follow a loaded car back to D.C.; and if anything goes down, do what you do too take the focus off them, and be out. I'll hit you wit a few Gs for the ride I-Iight! Sha' say I-Iight. I got you, whenever you ready. Omega says I'll let you know tonight. I'll holla at you then. Omega calls Rob and Tic and say, yo' what's good. Rob say, what's good player? Omega says everything from this side. Rob says same here. I'm going fishing tomorrow, you with dat? Omega says, oh' fo'sho. But I need to borrow one of your poles. Remember I told you I might need to borrow one? Rob says, yeah, I got you. I'll send it to you; just get it back to me in one piece. Omega says, no doubt! Yo' I got a solution for your pest problem. Rob says, say word! Omega says, yeah. When we get up, I'll holla at you bout it I-Iight! Rob says I-Iight then. My peoples will hit you when they touch. Omega says, I heard, 'ONE.' Omega and Rob never talked direct business on the phone. So the conversation they just had, they told each other that they were ready to do business. The driver was going to hit him up when she reaches Jersey; and the paid assassin wasn't going to be that far behind her. Omega was going to show him how to lock the block down that was off the chain. In so many words, in the next few days, there was going to be a lot of business, a lot of money made, and a lot of murder.

"LATER ON THAT NIGHT"

Ma'lik and Omega see each other in front of building 2. Ma'lik says' what's bangin' Mega? He says, you, me, the pound. Ma'lik say's that's what's up. You wanted to holla at me about something? Omega says, yeah. I need you to do something for me. I got someone coming from out of town too put some work in; and I need you to back him up and get him back here safe. It pays 10 grand, you up? Ma'lik says, no doubt! When is it gonna pop off? Omega says, this weekend. Ma'lik says o.k. Consider it done. Omega says, Ma'lik! No cowboy shit! I need it done very quick and very quite. Ma'lik says, I heard, you got dat homey.

END OF CHAPTER XXVIII

CHAPTER XXIX

"VENDETTA"

Sheeka lies in the bed, fucked up in the head. She can't believe her girl Mira is dead. She doesn't know why! But she has a gut feeling that Treeba and Vita had something to do with it. She curses them to hell; and promises that she'll find out and get revenge for her girl no matter what. 'She'll ride or die.' Mira was her only true friend; she loved her like a sister. They all grew up in the projects together. However, some cliques together; and some didn't. There's jealousy amongst some of the cliques in the hood, because they can't get it like the others. This set of girls didn't get along at all. Mira genuinely liked Omega. However, Omega knew that she was a goldigger. Zee liked him also; and she was more of a good girl, so she had a better chance. She was just too shy to let Omega know, that's why the 2 cliques had heat against each other. Sheeka was trying to concoct a plan. She decided she'd start hanging with K'mar's boys' girlfriends. They didn't like Treeba, Vita, and the others anyway. They use to beef with them at the rink, clubs, etc. Anywhere they would see them; it would almost, always, pop off. That's how much they hated each other. Sheeka started to cry. She called Fury's girlfriend and told her what was up. Fury's girl told her to come over to her house in Passaic whenever she was ready. When Sheeka showed up, all of the girls that were in the house showed her love, handled their business, brought her in; and embraced her. Now she was part of the family.

"ON ANOTHER PART OF TOWN"

It was Thursday; Omega had received the beep he was waiting for. He went to the secluded spot and met the driver. She was a white woman, professional looking. She looked like a collage professor, tall, very nice figure and bedroom eyes. Omega was instantly attracted to her. However, he always kept business, business. He says, hi! How are you? She says, fine! My name is Laura. He says, my name is Omega. She says, I know. I heard a lot of good things about you. The bags are in the trunk. Excuse the woman's clothing; we had to make things look good. He says no problem. He tells her to follow him, so she does. They pull into a garage. He has a few dudes waiting there to load the car. He says would you like to go get some dinner or something, before we take you to the hotel. Because the car isn't going to be ready until tomorrow. So you'll be leaving out tomorrow night sometime o.k. She says, fine. I am kinda hungry. They leave to go eat at the tavern on the green. As much as he wanted to push up on Laura, he knew that business and pleasure didn't mix. And it could have been as easy as just asking her, because she acted like she was big on him as well. They got to the restaurant. This was a five star restaurant, so the waiters kept your glasses full; and catered too you're every request. It was one of the 'hot spots.' Laura says this is a very elegant place. Omega says, yeah! Only the grown and sexy come here to eat. Then he smiles and she blushes. Omega says, so Laura, if you don't mind me asking, how did you hook up with Rob and Tic? She says, well! I know Rob from school, 'Howard.' We use to see each other, if you know what

I mean! However, we haven't been together in a minute. But we are still good friends. He does favors for me, and I do favors for him. Omega says, hmmm! That's what's up. We are still very close. I know what he does, but he helps me out a lot. Besides that, I don't do this on the regular; it's just a favor this one time. He has another driver; she's out of town right now. Omega says, so what do you do? She says, I have a degree in political science and I am a consultant for a large brokerage firm. Omega say, WOW! I wish you were a very good friend of mine. She smiles and says, I can be, anything's possible. I can also show you how to invest your money, clean it, and make it legal. Omega says, that's what I'm talking bout. I like you already. J-Gun says me too. I need to definitely holla at her. Are you into that Wall Street stuff? She says, yes! That's what I do. I can definitely make your money work for you. J-Gun says, I know I have to buy a certain amount of units, but how fast would we see our money flip? She says, it depends. Stock goes up and down every day. You just have to make sure your investment increases more than it decreases. I have made some lucrative investments for Tic and Rob. They are doing very well; and I would like to do the same for you two. That's another reason why I really came on this trip. Omega couldn't help himself. He said you have very beautiful eyes, they are green right? She says, yes! They are. J-Gun knew what was up, he kept laughing too himself, because he knew that if Omega slipped, she was going to get fucked lovely before she left Jersey. He was hoping that he didn't, but that was his homey, he knew how he was. They had finished eating and Omega asks her, is there anything else you would like to do while you're here? She says, no, I come up this way very often, but I be in New York most of the time, conducting business. So it's not like I don't know about up here. I am very tired from the drive though, where am I staying? He says wherever you want. She say, I don't care, just as long as I can take a nice, hot shower; and go to sleep in a nice, comfortable bed. Omega says o.k. I got you. He took her to the Embassy Suites hotel.

Checked her in. And as bad as he wanted to stay with her, he didn't. He told her; if you need me, just call, and I'll be here. She says o.k. However, in her head, she didn't really want him to leave. We'll be back early tomorrow o.k. She says, alright; and they left. When they got back to the car. J-Gun says I know that was hard. Omega says, more than you know. Maybe some other time. Right now, we have to make sure this thing works out, "no distractions."

The next day, Omega was awakened by a ring of his cell phone. Hello? Mega, everything is green, were waiting on you. He says, I-Iight, cool, give me a minute. The voice over the phone says, I-Iight, 'one.' He gets up and takes a shower in a big ass house that he lives at alone. He has four pit bulls that are 24-hour security. He calls J-Gun, 'J' you up? J-Gun says, yeah. I've been up fucking with this computer for a minute. Omega says, we gonna ride out in about an hour. He says I-Iight. You want me to drive or are you gonna drive. Omega says, you drive. J-gun says, I-Iight, I'll be thru. I-Iight, E.S. J-Gun finishes up on the computer and jumps in his Navigator. He then shoots to Englewood NJ and pulls up at Omega's house. He pushes the intercom. Omega sees that it's him and opens the gate. When he pulls around to the door, he steps out of the car and the dogs recognize him right away and greet him waging their tails. He opens the front door and yells 'yo!' where you at? Omega yells, I'm coming down now. Then he appears out of a room on the second floor. He walks down the stairs and gives J-Gun some dap and a hug. What's good homeboy? He says, you, me, the hood. Omega says, the car is ready, but we're gonna go holla at Sha' and make sure he is ready. She ain't gonna leave out until tonight anyway. J-Gun says I-Iight then. Your gonna invite her back up here, aren't you. Omega say, true story. I ain't gonna fuck with her now, because we're doing business. But when she comes back up here, its gonna be on and poppin.' You ready. Let's roll out. They jump in the car and roll out. They make their way to Paterson NJ.

In the projects, they see Sha' Omega says to him, what's good Sha'. You ready to roll? He says, yeah, just let me know when, its gonna be me and Rome. Omega say, about 12 tonight, be here Sha' this is business. He says, I got you mega. Omega says, I-light, I'll holla at you later then. Then he calls Laura, hello. He says, what's up. She says, nothing, just about to get something to eat. Omega says, get ready, we'll swing around and take you out for breakfast. She says o.k. I'll be down stairs. He says, cool, see you in a minute. She says, bye, in a low seductive voice. After a few minutes of driving, Omega and J-Gun pull up in the hotel. Laura jumps in and says, hi! They both say, hi. Omega says, what you in the mood for? She says, I'm in the mood for something long and hard; then she smiles. J-Gun laughs and so does Omega. Then she says, but for now, I'll take some grits, eggs, and fish. Omega says; let me find out you up on the soul food. She says I've been up on the soul food. Omega takes her to a soul food spot in Paterson, where the food is off the chain. They sit, order, and eat. Omega says will you be ready to leave out about 11. She says, yes. I'm ready, whenever you're ready. He says we're ready now! We just like to travel late night; you won't hit too much traffic. She says o.k. But what will I do until then? He says whatever! She says why don't you come back to the room and keep me company until then. He laughs and says to her, I would love too, but I can't. She says what! You're trying to be loyal to your wife or something? He says, no, I'm not married. I just don't like to mix business with pleasure. But if you were to come up again and it didn't pertain to business, I'm all yours. She say, well I'll have to make it back to Jersey real soon. Omega says I'll leave that up to you. She says I would like to go to the diamond district in New York and pick up something I seen there a few weeks ago. Omega says o.k. Fine. We'll go over there. Make a day out of it. I need to pick up something too.

END OF CHAPTER XXIX

CHAPTER XXX

"CRITICAL"

In building 8, a man and woman are going at it like 2 rabbits in heat. They had sex in the living room, in the kitchen, and the bathroom; they had sex practically all over the apartment. They are trying to outdo each other. The young lady is usually quiet. However, she refuses to submit and give in to her lover. The young man is a beast on the street and more of a beast in the bed. He's trying to string the young woman out. However, he has met his match, because the more he gives, the more she wants. After every episode they have had, they both leave speechless and they fall harder for each other. As they lay soak and wet and exhausted in the bed, Ma'lik sees the scares on Vita's back. He softly touches it and says, "I'm sorry." Vita says, for what? He rubs on the scare and says, for this! She says its o.k. He says, no! It's not. I was young and reckless. I had no sense at all; and I shot you, because your brother wasn't there. I use to hate y'all asses, but today I feel different. Y'all are good people; your brother is a good dude. Vita says, it's alright Ma'lik, I forgive you, "trust me" I do. Vita is thinking that if she hadn't forgiving him, he'd be a target right now. She loved him on the low. She wouldn't dare tell him that though. Ma'lik asks her, are you alright? You need anything? She says, no, I'm o.k. He says, here, take this anyway just in case; and hands her a knot of money. On the low, Ma'lik was loving her too. He couldn't believe that someone he once shot and tried to kill, he was in love with. She says, Ma'lik, I don't want to take all of your money. He says. That's nothing, I got more. She says, you just got home, you need your money. He says, for real, keep it. I want you to have it. I got more and Omega is gonna hit me off with some more, so I'm good. She says o.k. But I don't want you to think that I'm sexing you for your money. He says, I know, but I feel like I owe it to you for what I did. She hugs him and say, look! You don't owe me nothing o.k. Remember that. And I'm with you because I wanna be. Ma'lik looks at her, and for the first time in his life, the always hard, always killer attitude, always the tough guy, felt like a soft ass punk, because he was in love.

"LATER ON, IN THE FRONT OF THE POUND"

Its 11: 30, Omega is on the cell phone with Sha'. Omega says, Sha' pick me up something to eat from that restaurant that I like. Sha' says, I got you, 'ONE.' That was code for; go meet with the car and ride out. Omega calls Laura and says, give em' a minute; and I'll see you, when I see you o.k. She says which will be soon. He says o.k. And they both say bye. After a while, Sha' meets up with Laura and they head out for Washington D.C. It's raining, stormy, and wet. Laura is driving slow since it's wet and slippery. Sha' and Rome are following about 6 to 7 cars behind, keeping a safe distance. Rome has a lead foot, so sometimes he catches little races on the highway, playing around, then falling back again when his radar detector goes off for police. Today he drove somewhat normal, because of the rain. They were 2 hours into the road trip when a police car got behind Laura and hit his lights. She pulls over. Sha' and Rome see the police car pull her over, so they pull over as if they were having car trouble. They were about 15 car lengths behind them. Watching and acting as if they were checking the car. The police officer asks Laura for her license, insurance, and registration. She flirts with the officer and asks him, "What seems to be the problem officer?" Laura looks like a collage professor, very professional and very important. The officer says one of your taillights is out. She says, really! May I see? He says, yes. So she gets out. Then she and the officer walk to the back of the car. The light is out. She hits it, it comes back on. She says, there it go. The cop says, yeah! You probably have a short in the wire or something. She says I did hit a big pothole, so maybe that did it. I will be sure to get it checked out when I get back home. I am just coming back from giving a dissertation at NYU. He says, really! You must be tired. She says, yes, but I can manage. I drive like this all the time. He says, here; and hands her, her paper work back. Get the lights checked and drive safely o.k. She says o.k. I will thank you. He say's "You're welcome" and walks back to his car. She gets back into the car and drives off. The police sees Sha' and Rome having car trouble, so he makes a U-turn and tries to assist them. They run some bullshit on him about the car stalling. He asks do you need a tow truck? Sha' says, no' it does this sometime. It overheats. After it cools down, it'll be alright. The cop says, alright; and drives off. Now Laura has about 20 minutes on them, so they got too catch up. Rome starts to speed to catch her. Sha' tells him, yo! Slow down before you lose control of the car. (Sha' felt the car hydroplaning) Rome says, chill Sha' I got this. Just sit back and relax; and he kept speeding. He was changing lanes recklessly. All of a sudden, 'SWUUURT BOOOOM! He loses control of the car; and then it was complete darkness. About 15 minutes later, Rome and Sha' was brought back to consciousness by the Medics. They pulled Rome out of the car and Sha' tries to move, but he couldn't. It was as if a 2-ton weight was holding him down. He didn't know what was wrong with him. But the reality was, he was paralyzed from the waist down. As the

Medics pulled him from the burning car, he realized that the car was wrapped around a tree, like an apron wrapped around a chef's body. The car was hugging the tree; it's a miracle that they were alive. A helicopter had to lift them off to a hospital, for they were in critical condition. Rome was all broken up, and in shock. Sha' had fallen out again. Laura had gotten to D.C. safely. However, she wondered what had happened to Rome and Sha'. (Only if she knew that they were lying up in surgery rooms, holding on for dear life.)

END OF CHAPTER XXX

CHAPTER XXXI

"THE LETTER"

Omega goes to his aunt's house. She tells him he has mail. He gets the letter; it's from Big Dixie.......

What's good youngin' I heard you doing your thing out there, just be safe and cover all of your tracks. Don't let nobody know what you're doing. Everybody is suspect, even your momma. The game is dirty; there's nothing fair about it, "remember that." I appreciate you looking out for my babies, 'that's love right there' I'm feeling you for that. That's why I made the decision to put you down on something. I use to deal with your mother before she died; and before you were born. Your mother and me had a thing going on. She was a good woman. Before she died, she told me, to tell you, that you were my son. I know this is some heavy shit to lay on you right now. And I've been wanted to tell you, but your aunt told me not too for your well being. That's why I use to have you around me all the time. I want you to know that I loved your mother. I still do, but I had a wife back then, so that's why things had to go down the way they did. So now, you know; and now you know that Monty and Treecy is your little brother and sister. If you don't believe me ask your aunt and make her tell you the truth. Now there's something else I want to lay on you that's gonna be heavy. I have another daughter from a woman that lives in the Hampton's. She black and Chinese. Her family is very rich; they own some Companies in China. 'Look' she's gonna bring you a key to a storage spot up in Wayne, its on Clear Ave. Go get that, go get my babies, and take care of them for me until they can take care of themselves. I know I might be asking for a lot, but your family and I need you to do this for me. As far as their mother is concerned, handle that for me. Very quiet like, feel me! She gonna die fucking with that shit anyway, but I can't forgive her for putting my babies through that abomination. I took care of that woman for a very long time, I trusted her to take care of my children, and she didn't. She scarred them for life. The woman I need you to get in touch with, her name is Misa; and my baby girl name is Keenu. You're little sister. She's about 7 now. You can reach her at 1917-555-1123. She will be expecting your call o.k. I know I can count on you to do this for me. I'm gonna continue to fight these mutha' fucka's to the end. Putting in appeals, trying to get sentence reduction etc. Maybe one day I'll see you on the streets again 'one day'... Omega get what you can and get out. You can't put a set date on it. You just have to leave it. Turn it over to someone and never look back; or you'll end up like me. And I don't want that. I want better for you and the rest of my children. So think about that real, real hard youngin' you still got a chance. Do something legal with that doe alright! Until next time, love is love, I'm out.

You're Pops,
Big Dixie

Omega turns to his aunt and says auntie! Is Big Dixie my father? She looks at Omega with pain in her eyes. She says, I knew you were gonna ask me that one day. And I said to myself, if you were old enough, I wouldn't lie to you, so yes, he is. He took a blood test when your mother first had you in the hospital. He was there for the delivery too. He just didn't tell anybody about it, because of his wife. I didn't like him, because I knew he was seeing lots of woman. And I knew how he made a lot of his money. I didn't like it, but I had to deal with it, because of you and my sister. Just like I know what you do. But I deal with it, because I love you. I pray for you everyday Omega! Hoping you would stop and not end up like your father, because you're heading down the same road. With the drugs, with the woman, money, and god knows whatever else. I'm not going to preach to you. I know you have god in your life, but now you have to find your own way. You'll have to live a normal life, but you'll live. As long as you're in that type of business, you're slowly dying. I dread the thought of receiving a call one-day of someone telling me you're dead. I would lose my mind, you hear me! I couldn't take that. You are my only nephew; you're all I got and I do not want to lose you. So please! Do the right thing. Omega is full of pain; because he knows what his aunt is telling him is true. He knows there's a lot of love there; because of the pain he feels when she talks to him. Her words always hit him like 50 cal bullets. He says, auntie I'm a get it right, I promise. I'm doing some other things, so I don't have to hustle too much longer. You'll see, I'll make you proud; and gives her a kiss on the forehead. He says, you alright! You need something, anything. She says, no baby! I don't want your money. He says I got a surprise for you for your birthday. She says, you don't have to do that, I'm fine. He says, no auntie, you deserve it. You work very hard. You need something nice and I'm a get it for you and that's it. I'm gone! And as he leaves he sneaks and places a brick of money in her pocketbook, jumps in his Benz and takes off. His cell phone rings. Its J-Gun he says, 'yo' Rome and Sha' was in a bad accident. They're in the hospital and they're really fucked up. They said Sha' may not walk again, because his spine popped. And Rome broke his leg, his arm, his hip, and he fucked up his face a little. Omega says, damn! Did Laura make it back? He says, yeah, she's good. She called to find out what happened to them. Then I got a call from Sha's moms. She told me what happened. They were speeding, lost control of the car, and smashed into a tree. Omega says, I-light, we gotta go see them as soon as we can. J-Gun says, Sha's moms says there gonna be down there a couple of days, then their gonna get moved to a spot up in West Orange. Omega says, I-light, we'll wait until they get there, then go see em. What's up with Sweets and them? J-Gun says their I-light. They got rid of like a quarter of the shit, but ain't no problems. You saw Treecy and Monty? He says, nah, not today. O.k. if you see them, give them some money for me. A face apiece I-light! He says, I-light, I got you. Omega says I have to go do something real quick. Then I'll come snatch you up, and let you know what's goody I-light! 'One'. Then Omega dials up the number Big Dixie gave him. 'Ring, ring,' hello? A soft seductive, sensual voice answers the phone. Hello! Can I speak to Misa? She says, speaking. Then he hears a young voice in the background. Mama! Is that my father? She says, no honey, not yet. The young child says, ah'man, he is taking too long to call. I want to talk to him very bad. Misa says, I know honey. He will call in a minute. She says, I am sorry. Who is this? He says, omega. She says, oh' hi. I was waiting for you to call. Dixie told me to expect your call. Omega says that must be Keenu in the background. She says, yes. We are waiting on her father to call. Every time the telephone rings, she thinks it's her father. Omega says sounds like she loves him. She says, more than anything in this world, he is all she talks about. You're calling for the key right! He says, yes. She says you are in New Jersey right! If you want, I can meet you. He says, no! If you don't mind, I'll ride up by you; I need to take a ride to get away for awhile. She says o.k. I'm in the Hampton's. When you get here, call me back and I will direct you to the house. He says o.k. See you then, bye. She says, bye. Omega wanted to see the

Hamptons anyway. He heard that it was beautiful up there. Now he had a reason to go see for himself. After about a 3 hours of driving. He saw a sign that said, "Welcome to the Hamptons" so he called her back and said, hello? Misa. She says, yes. He says I'm in town; I just turned off the exit. She says, o.k. Drive straight thru town, make a right at the light, then a left, and come straight on down. You will see an alcove, when you get to the gate I'll let you in. He says o.k. I'm almost there; I'm at the alcove. O.K. I'm in front of the gate. She presses a button, and the gate opens. Her house is a beautiful mansion. Out front, there's a 2009 CL65 Benz, X5 BMW, and a Bentley coupe. He admires her taste. He sees that she is at the front door and her daughter is by her side. He smiles, because the little girl is the spitting image of her father, Big Dixie. He parks the car and steps out. He walks to the door, says hi to Misa, and shakes her hand. Then he turns to Keenu and says, hi pretty girl. She says, 'hi' in a soft voice and smiles. Misa says, come in, would you like something to drink? He says some juice would be nice. Misa says I have apple, orange, or cran-apple. He says cran-apple please. He looks around. He thinks to himself, WOW! Because she has expensive paintings hanging up, along with pictures of the family. A picture of her, Big Dixie, and Keenu when she was an infant. A few pictures of her, her mother, and her father, she's a teenager in the picture. A family portrait of her two brothers, her sister, and her parents in China. She has all kinds of Oriental statues. Life-size Samurai statues, humongous Chandeliers, a giant fireplace, and Italian marble floors. The Mansion has 32 rooms, 25 bathrooms, and 5 full kitchens. She has 2 nannies, 2 Chauffeur, 1 Butler, 4 Chefs, and 6 all purpose workers and house cleaners. They have been with her family for years, so they are all loyal and trustworthy, to her, her daughter, and Big Dixie. The maid brings him his drink. He says, thank you. Omega is intrigued from Misa's beauty. He thinks to himself that she can't be no older than 30. However, she stands about 6ft tall, about 140pds co-co butter tone and long silky hair. She kind of favors, 'kamora Lee Simmons.' She goes in her Jean pocket, pulls out a key, and hands it to Omega. He says, thank you. She says I would like to meet Monty and Treecy. I want Keenu to meet her brothers and sister and know who they are. It's what Dixie wants, and I can't stop that. In fact, I encourage it. I love Dixie with all of my heart and soul. And whatever he wants, I try to do for him. He's a good-hearted man, and he's a good father. He use to tell me all the stories about the projects, the life he lived, and how he wanted to make it much easier for his children. And not have them struggle like he did when he was growing up. I knew all about his other families. Vicki and her children, you and your mother, but I decided to accept it. He use to tell me how much he loved kids and he wanted as many as he could take care of. He has always been honest with me. He says that he only has 4 children. You, Keenu, Monty, and Treecy. I believe him, because he did not have to tell me about y'all. I want you to know that, you are always welcome here, all three of you. And I'm not going to stop helping your father fight his appeals, and whatever else he does to try to get free again o.k. Omega smiles and says, he is very lucky to have someone like you on his side. And if there is anything, I can do to help you, just call me o.k. She says o.k. He says, we'll I have to be going; I got a long ride back. So he gives her a hug; and gives Keenu a hug and starts for the door. Misa says, Omega be careful and don't be a stranger. He says o.k. And I'll make sure to keep in touch.

"AFTER A FEW HOURS"

J-Gun's cell phone rings. He sees that it's Omega from the caller ID. He says, what's good homey? Omega says, what's good, 'yo' meet me by the Brownstone in about a half. J-Gun says, I-Iight, what's up? He says, I don't know, I'll let you know what's good when I see you. J-Gun says, I-Iight, I'll be there. After about a half-hour, Omega pulls up in the Brownstone; J-Gun is sitting there already.

He pulls along side of him, and J-Gun jumps in his car and leaves his car parked. Omega says, we're gonna go to the storage spot up in Wayne real quick. I got something up there I have to go get. They drive to the storage spot. They drive up to a gate that has a code box on the side of it. He pulls out the key and there's numbers on it. On one side, there's 1301. So he presses it in on the box and the gate opens. On the other side, there's a 15 on it. So he drives garage 15 and it's a big door, a garage door. He uses the key and opens the garage. When he opens it, he sees a burgundy drop top Bentley. They walk in, J-Gun says, yo! This shit is beaten' I never seen this. Omega says, it's Big Dixie's. J-Gun says, Damn! He never drove this in the hood; they would've locked his ass up just for driving this shit. Omega says, true story. He opens the door to the car, and sees the keys to the car, in the car. He starts it up. It turns over, and it runs like a cat purring. He pops the trunk and sees 2 large suit cases. He opens one and it's full of money. Then he opens the other, and it's full of cocaine and 2 solid gold desert eagles. They look custom made. J-Gun says, WOW!!! B.D. had this stash for a rainy day 'hunh'. Omega says this probably was run money or security money for his children or something. He tells J-Gun to go to the office and ask them how much money is due on lot 15, so he does. Omega puts the bags in his car while J-Gun goes to the office. When J-Gun gets back, he says that the lot has been paid off for the year. Omega assumes that Misa must have been keeping up on the bill for the storage lot. He turns the Bentley off and locks the garage door. They jump in the car and take off. They drive back to J-Gun's car. Omega says, take the coke up top. I'm a make some calls and try to off it real quick. Call O'l boy in Passaic and see if he wants to cop any. Tell him we'll give him a deal. The more he buys, the more we'll work with him. I'm a go put this money up; and I'll meet you in the P.Js. J-Gun says, I-Iight, and spins off. Omega goes to his house in Englewood; and puts the bag of money in the floor safe that he has hidden in his walk in closet. Then he remembers that he has to see Treecy and Monty. And that he has to handle the situation with their mother. He jumps back in his car and heads to the projects. As he riding down route 4, he gets a ring on his cell. It's J-Gun. He answers, what's good dawgy. J-Gun says, where you at? He says, on my way there, why what's up? J-Gun says, come straight here, Vicki's dead. I'll tell you the rest when you get here. Omega says, I-Iight, give me a minute, 'One.' Omega speeds up a little, but not too much, because the police on route 4 are quick to pull you over, **"They be buggin."** He gets to the projects and everybody is standing around. He sees J-Gun, Treecy, and Monty standing in the back parking lot. Treecy is crying her eyes out, but Monty shows no emotion what so ever. He's just standing there, quite. Omega walks up and Treecy just hugs him and cries some more. He says, don't worry, y'all are going to be alright. He looks at J-Gun and says, what happen? He says, Treecy said she's been missing since last night. Then the maintenance man goes to fix up one of the abandoned apartments and finds her dead with a needle next to her. Omega is fucked up from the news, but at the same time relieved. Big Dixie wanted him to take her out, because of the abomination she was putting his kids through; and he really didn't want her death on his hands. He wouldn't know how to explain that to Monty and Treecy, if they ever found out. He says to himself, it was her time. The lord must of seen that it was no reason to keep her on this earth, so his will had to be done. Omega tells Treecy and Monty to go get their things from the apartment. All the stuff they wanted to keep, because they were coming home with him. He calls over two crack heads and tells them to help them with their things, and he'll look out for them when they are finished. They were glad to help Omega, because they knew he would hit them off decent after the job was done. He gave Treecy some money and told her to go to the laundry mat and buy some of those nylon bags to put their stuff in. Then bring it down stairs, and put it in the truck. While they are up stairs, Officer Steele and Officer Mendez pull up.

He calls Omega to the side. Where are Treecy and Monty? He says, they are up stairs packing their things, don't worry! I got' em. Steele looks at him concerned and says you sure? Omega says, yeah. Big Dixie wants me to take care of them for him. Steele says, alright, because I don't want family services to step in and try to split them up and put them in a foster home, they need each other. If you need anything, some help with them call me. Omega says I-light. Steele and Mendez jump back into the unmarked car and drive off.

"A FEW DAYS LATER"

At the funeral, everyone is standing around, mourning and dressed in black. It's drizzling slightly; there are mad flowers around the casket and lots of crying. It's a sad scene. All of Vicki's family and friends are grieving her death. In the front are Treecy, Monty, Omega, and Devon. The tombstone reads, Vicki Veora Steele Dixon. Beloved wife, Beloved mother, and friend to all. **D.O.B. 2-12-1965, D.O.D. 4-20-2005.** After the funeral services, Devon Steele stands by the car talking to his niece and nephew, Treecy and Monty. He say's to them "y'all are going to be alright, you're going to be staying with their brother Omega. Treecy and Monty looked shocked and say, "Brother" Omega is our brother? Steele says, yes, that's your father's son by another woman. He'll explain it to you. If y'all need me, you have my number. Treecy hugs her uncle Steele and Monty says I-light unc. Then he goes to Omega and says, take care of them, they have been through a lot. Also you need to start doing the right thing for them, and yourself, you don't want to end up like Dixie. You are all they have now; they don't want to live with me. Also if I were you! I wouldn't be in those projects, Saturday or Sunday. Omega listen to me, give it up. Take your money and do something else with it. Start a business or something, because the time they are giving out now! It's not worth it. Omega says, I'm working on something now to get out Steele, I really am! It just takes a little time, but I'm a let it go real soon. Steele says, soon is too long. You just have to stop, because if you set a date that date will never come. You will keep saying, o.k. I'm a quit after this last flip, then that flip will be fast and smooth and that will lead to about a hundred last flips, and you will stay sucked in, I've seen it a million times. Just leave it and don't look back, that's the best way. Omega says, I hear you Steele. Steele says, alright! Then he walks over to his niece and nephew; gives them a hug and leaves. J-Gun walks up to Omega and say, everything alright? He says, yes, everything's good. Shop is closed this weekend. We'll just off the coke, but tell everybody to chill, Friday, Saturday and Sunday. We'll go get whatever they make Thursday and stash the work until Monday or Tuesday. Take the coke to the other spot just in case they raid the buildings. J-Gun says, I-light, I'll tell Shim and Big Sex to move it. At that moment, Omega gets a call on his cell phone. He answers the phone, hello? The voice says in a soft seductive tone, hey stranger! He recognizes the voice and says, hey! 'L' boogie, what's good lovely. She says you and me this weekend. He says, sounds good to me. You gonna make a trip up here just to see me? She says, not just you, I have some business I have to take care of in the city. But I have to be there, Friday until Monday. I'm going to leave back out Monday night. He says o.k. I'll get us a spot for the days you're here. She says I hope you don't have any plans this weekend, because I want you all to myself, I have plans for you. He says you're in luck. Something came up, so I'm all yours. She says, good. I'll be there Friday about 6pm. I will call you when I get there. I will be there earlier, but I have to go to Wall Street. I should be done by 5 or 6 o.k. He says o.k. Laura says, I'll see you then baby, bye. He says bye; they hang up. Omega says, 'J' you gonna take care of that for me? I have to take Treecy and Monty to the furniture store and get a few things. I'm a holla at you in a minute and come thru I-light. J-Gun say, I-light, I'll holla, E.S. They give each other dap, jump in their cars and drive off.

END OF CHAPTER XXXI

CHAPTER XXXII

"BE ON POINT"

Downtown Newark' Vita, Treeba, and Zee are clothes shopping, going store-to-store, spending money. They love shopping; it's like an addiction. They buy things on sale and at full price. They walk out of Dr Jays and they notice a blue Excursion following them. It has limo-tinted windows, so they can't see who's driving. Vita says, that's the second time I seen that truck drive slow by us, it look like that fool K'mar's truck. They walk into a shoe store and the truck speeds off. Zee says dag! What's that about? Treeba says, I don't know girl, but that nigga be trippin'. Let's just get the rest of this shit, and go. Zee gets 2 pair of shoes. Vita and Treeba get their boots. They pay for them and walk out the store. Waiting for them was the blue truck. Zee says, what is wrong with this fool. They walk towards the parking lot, where the car is parked. The truck moves slowly with them. Treeba stops and says what nigga! What the fuck! The windows from the truck roll down, its Sheeka. She says, brace y'all self cause y'all some dead bitches now! Then there's rapid gunfire from the truck. Treeba, Zee, and Vita are shook and they start to hall ass, screaming, and all. The truck speeds off. No one is hit. However, the girls are very confused and hysterical. Treeba says, no this bitch didn't! I'm a kill that bitch when I see her. Zee is in shook and Vita is emotionless. She's just standing there zoned out. The reason why no one was hit is, because the passengers were shooting in the air. Their intentions were to scare the shit out of them, and they succeeded. The girls knew that they had to be on point from now on. They gathered their things, jumped in the car, and headed home.

"FRIDAY"

It's Friday, and Karma was clothes shopping in the mall. She was in the Dolce & Gabana store. She was approached by a man while shopping. He says you have real expensive taste shorty. She says you only live once, so you have to make the best of it, and wear the best. He says, I feel you. Haven't I seen you somewhere before? I know it sounds corny, but I have. She replies, maybe at the clubs. Sometimes I like to go out every now and then. He says which clubs? She says, Paradise, Cheetah, The Rink, I be all over. I like to have a good time. He says, is that right. She says, yup! That's right. He says, what's your name lovely? She says, Madi. He says, nice to meet you, my name is Ka'mar; and they shake hands. He says, since you like to have a nice time, maybe I can take you out sometime. She says, maybe. He says; give me your number, so I can call you. She says, I tell you what, give me yours, and when I plan on going out, I'll call you. He says, fair enough; and he gives her the number. She puts the clothes that she picked out, on the register. K'mar says let me get that for you mama. She says I can pay for my own stuff. He says, I know; just take it as an incentive to call me. And hands the cashier a couple of franky faces and says to Madi, this is nothing. You want to have a good time, call me; I'll show you how to have a good time. She says, o.k. Balla, I got you. He kisses her hand and says I'll be waiting on your call. Then he says bye, and leaves the store. Outside of the store, his boys were waiting on him. He joins them and says shorty is hot as hell! I gots to bag that. You see the body on her; she is the truth. All his comrades agree with what he's saying as they walk off. Back at the store, Karma gathers her bags and head for the mall exit. Then makes a call on her cell phone. Yeah papi, I finally ran into that fool, so it's about to go down. Do what you got to do and I'll keep you posted o.k. Papa, I'll call you later, bye. On the other end of the phone, the person calls his boy and say, yeah! What's good how's everything? He says, everything's lovely. More than lovely. He says, that's good. "Yo" I'm a need you to send O'l boy up in a minute; I'll let you know exactly when. He says, enough said, just let me know and he'll hit you when he get there, I-Iight playa. Omega says, I-Iight, 'One.

Laura calls omega, hey boo! What's up? Omega say, hey lovely where you at? She says I'm just leaving New York; I'm on the G.W.B. He says, good, hit route 3, I got us a spot in the Marriott. Go to the desk and tell them your name and they'll give you the key. As soon as I finish my business, I'll be there. Give me about an hour o.k. She says o.k. Boo. He says, you o.k. You need anything? She says; just bring yourself, that's all I need. I got us some Champagne already and we can order in. He says, I-Iight, I'll be there in a minute. She says o.k. Bye. He says, bye. Then omega calls Shim-Shawn and Big Sex and say's to them "round up the guap y'all made and put the rest of the work up till next week. Shim-Shawn says I-Iight. Omega says, leave the guap at the other spot; I'll be there to get it in a minute. He says, I-Iight, 'One'. Omega calls his house in Englewood to check on Treecy and Monty. Treecy answers the phone, hello? Omega says, Hey Tre what's up. She says nothing. I'm on the phone with my girlfriend and chatting on the computer. Omega says, where's Monty? She says, I don't know. He was playing with the dogs, but then someone pulled up in a car, blew the horn and he left. Omega says, are you alright, you hungry? She says, no, but I would like some ice cream, I ate already. He says what kind? She says strawberry. He says o.k. I'll be there in a minute. She says o.k. And they hang up. Then he calls J-Gun, Hello, 'J' what's good. He says, you. Omega says, 'yo' Laura is up here, so I'm gonna be chillin with her at the Marriott. What you getting into? J-Gun says, nothing much. I'm a get at shorty for a while then take it down. Omega says, I-Iight, cool. We're gonna be easy till Monday, so this is a fall back weekend ya' heard. I was thinking about hitting the rink tomorrow, you wit dat? J-Gun says, yeah, I'm wit it. Omega says, I-Iight, I'll holla back, 'One'. J-Gun says, 'One'. Omega goes to the spot he has out of the projects and picks up the money Shim and Big Sex dropped off. Locks the spot back up and heads for the ice cream parlor. He picks up some strawberry, butter pecan, and chocolate, and then he heads home. Once he gets there, he kisses Treecy on the forehead and says, hey shorty! She says, hey! Then he asks did you hear from your brother? She says, no, I was about to call him on his cell. Omega says o.k. When you speak to him, tell him not to stay out too late please. She says o.k. I'll tell him. Then he says, will you be o.k. I'll be gone until tomorrow morning. She says I'll be fine. If I can stay in them crazy projects alone all night, I can definitely stay here by myself. Besides, I have these big dogs here body guarding me; and she smiles. Then she says, big brah, I don't want you to stop living your life, because Monty and I are a part of it now. You don't have to baby sit us. I am 15 and he is 16, so we can do a lot of things on our own. We were taking care of ourselves when we were with mommy and we can manage now. So don't worry too much about us, we alright. We love you for doing for us and taking us in big brah, but we don't want to become a burden o.k. Omega looks at her in shock and says, I-Iight baby girl, you growing up on me; and gives her a kiss on the forehead again. Then he goes and puts the bag of money up. When he walked back into the dining room he says, I'm gonna take y'all to get some more clothes tomorrow, so make sure you call your brother and tell him 'not too late' o.k. And he walks for the door, jumps in the car, and drives off. He then calls Laura's cell phone and says, I'm on my way. She says o.k. Baby, I'll be waiting. He says, do me a favor and run me some hot water in the tub. She says they have a Jacuzzi tub in here; I'll fill it with hot water for you. He says I-Iight then. She says sounds like you need a good working over. I got you; I'm a take good care of you this weekend, massages and all. He says, sounds good, I'll see you in a minute. They hang up. After a while, he gets to the hotel and he jumps on the elevator, then knocks on the door. Laura opens the door in a pink Negligee set. She has a tan that makes her body look a co-co butter complexion; she looks like she just came from the beaches of Cali sun bathing. Her skin is flawless, not a wrinkle, stretch mark, or blemish in sight. Her titties stand at attention, begging to be caressed. Her nipples are like two baby pacifiers, pink and hard. Omega looks at her love box, it's so fat, it looks like its padded, but that's all her and its hairless. Omega loves a shaved pussy. He walks backwards, kissing and rubbing on her. He feels on her vagina and its soak and wet with the clit the size of an oversized grape. He rubs on it and after a minute she cums. She says, Omega I'm multi- orgasmic, so I cum like a flowing river. He says that's fine with me. I got a lot of stamina, so you're gonna be cumin a lot tonight. He rips her thong from around her waist, she screams slightly with pleasure. She grabs on his magic stick and start to rub on it, it starts to rise, it gets bigger, and bigger, three times its size. She says I want you inside of me. I want you to put all of this dick in me; and fuck my brains out. She unbuttons his paints and all of his manhood is standing straight up, she can't believe her eyes. She says, rip my clothes off and fuck me Omega, I like it rough. She begs him, "rip em off'" he obliges. He grabs her by her hair and say, you want it rough. You want this dick. She says, yeah baby, give it to me. He starts to rip the rest of her Negligee off. She says, yeah Baby! Take this pussy! He picks her up and carries her to the bed. Puts her down, turns her on her stomach with a little force; and smacks her, on her ass with his dick. She screams, "Ooh yeah Baby"! Then he slides his magic stick up and down her dripping wet pussy. She makes all kinds of animal like sounds, moans, and groans. He continues to tease her, smacking her on the ass. He wants to slay her, but he doesn't. He puts the head of his dick in; and kisses her on the back. She says, bite me Omega, "bite me" So he bites her gently and rubs on her breast. Then she says, stick it in, stop teasing me. So he sits up and puts his long, hard dick inside of her and she starts going crazy. Omega starts wildin' out on the pussy, drilling it like a pile driver. She starts screaming, "I'm cumin, I'm cumin." He bangs her harder and harder. She lets out a scream of pleasure and pain. Omega continues to go to work on her, digging into her deeper and deeper. She starts to cum again and again. By the time Omega starts to reach his climax, she had came about 10 to 12 times. Omega feels the rush in his rod. He starts to squint his eyes and continues to bang her pussy like he's trying to kill her sexually. She feels herself cumin again. Omega lets out a loud roar and cums so hard, until he screams with pain and pleasure and she does the same. So that makes 13 times she orgasms to his 1 long, hard Orgasm. They fall to the bed and fall asleep for awhile. About an hour later, Omega wakes up, he walks to the bathroom and pisses, then he looks in the mirror. He can't believe the sex he just had, he never came that hard before. He felt like he dumped a gallon of semen in her and he didn't use a condom. He was in bliss, and at the same time worried, because he just had the best-unprotected sex of his life. He didn't know Laura, she could be sick for all he knows. He lets the water out of the Jacuzzi tub and runs some fresh, hot water, and jump in. About 15 minutes later, he hears footsteps, its Laura. She jumps in the Jacuzzi with him and start to caress and rub on him. He has his eyes closed and he like what he feels. Laura starts to suck him off. He enjoys the feeling. As she devours his long, hard on, she plays with herself, and then she gets up and turns around. Omega tries to guide his hard on into her pussy, but she says, "No," she grabs it and guides it into her voluptuous ass. At first, it was hard getting it into her. However, after awhile of trying, it gradually inters her. She makes soft sounds of pleasure and pain. She is enjoying the sexual encounter that she is having with Omega. Omega is very experienced, so he knows how to please a woman. He puts in a lot of work when it comes to sex. After working it out in Laura's anus for awhile, Laura starts to get into it. She say's Omega "harder, harder baby, harder." Omega starts to dig in. She says, 'ooh yeah Baby' like that. I feel it, I'm about to cum, I'm about tooo, cuuuumm! Then she lets out a loud scream, "aaahhh." At that same time, Omega cums too. He yells, "Ahhh shit, fuck" and wipes the sweat off of his face. Laura smiles and grabs her heart. Then she says, I cannot believe I came while being fucked in the ass; and it felt sooo' good. I have been trying to do that for so long, now it finally happened; you are something else. Omega smiles and thinks to himself, another satisfied female, he's proud of himself. Laura grabs a washcloth and soap and starts to wash Omega. Omega lays back and enjoys the pampering. She washes herself and they dry each other off; and retire to the bed. They watch TV. Until they fall asleep.

"SATURDAY"

Its Saturday, everyone is piling up in their cars to go to 'The Rink.' The Rink is that spot right now, it's like a big fashion show. People show off their cars and clothes. They play dice and bet on all the little games that they have in the skating rink. Most of the women come to find a Balla they can hook up with, even if it's just for the night. The young ladies are dress to kill. They don't even have to look all that hot in the face, just as long as they got a fat ass, nails done, hair done, they will attract attention. Believe me when I tell you, they will be going home, to breakfast, or to a hotel with somebody! Omega and damn near the whole projects are in the Rink tonight. Along with all the money making blocks in Paterson. All of the blocks beef, one time or another. However, when the go out, they clique up. Therefore, if one person fights from Paterson, the whole Paterson fights. That goes for all the towns; they have the same rules also. People from all over are here, New Jersey, New York, Connecticut, Asbury, Plainfield, and Upstate; they come from all over. You have a lot of young ladies skating and having a nice time. Guys are Observing them, trying to holla. Some of the guys are skating; most of them aren't, because they don't know how, not because they don't want to and some are just too cool to skate. Skating is a sure way to get with a shorty. She'll help you skate, or you can help her. This particular night, Skip was skating around, enjoying himself, bugging with the ladies. A lot of them know him, some don't, however, they are still bugging with him. He trips over a well known, New York drug dealer's foot. He says, "Pardon me fam" Dude was like, what! Skip says, pardon me, my bad. The dealer says, yo' say it louder; you ain't say it loud enough. Now dude always roll with a gang of his boys, there was about 30 to 40 of them there. However, Skip was from the projects, he had heart and he put that work in; and he had the whole Paterson in the Rink that night. So his response was, "what nigga" I ain't say it loud enough, is this loud enough. **"FUCK YOU"** the dude from New York homeboys started posting up behind him. And Skip's homies were as deep as his were, so they started posting up behind him. The dude made a lot of that guap and him and his homeboys were heavy on the jewelry, Benz jackets, BMW jackets, and the whole nine, But so was Skip's boys, they were heavy with the same. So Skip says, what's poppin' nigga? What ya' wanna do? Pop off. The dude seen that Skip had a heavy crew; and that he would have got smashed out if it would have popped off. So he said 'nah' ain't nothing fam. Skip says, oh' now it ain't nothing. Then one of Skip's homies say, "you'se a fag, nigga" then throws juice in his face. Dude didn't want it, he didn't want it at all, so all he did was stare for a minute, then he told his boys let's go; and they spent off and left the Rink. I know dude felt some type of way, because he was that dude in New York, but over in Jersey, he had nothing coming. He wasn't no match for the niggas in Jersey.

END OF CHAPTER XXXII

CHAPTER XXXIII

"YOU'SE A DEAD MUTHA'FUCKA"

Omega receives a ring on his cell phone, it says pay phone on the caller I.D. The voice says Omega? He says, yeah! Who dis? The voice says this is Rob's boy. Omega says, oh' I-light, where you at? I'll come pick you up. He says I'm at McDonalds on a market street. Omega says o.k. I'll be there in a minute I-light. He says, I-light 'one.' Omega then calls Karma and says, hey Mama! Where you at? She says, I'm home. He says, look, I'm about to come thru. She says, alright papi, I'll be here. Omega then swings by Micky D's and sees Rob's boy sitting in a car, he signals him to follow him. He puts him up in a friend's apartment out of the projects. He tells him what he has to do and that someone is going to be with him. The guy says I-light. Then Omega say's to him I'll be back. Omega then leaves and goes to the projects. He sees Ma'lik out front and calls him to the car. He says, Ma'lik it's going down tonight, you ready? Ma'lik says I'm always ready homey. Omega says, do what you got to do and meet me out back in a half. He says I-light. Omega then parks the car and goes to Karma's apartment. He knocks; she opens the door, hey papi! And gives him a kiss on the cheek. He says, what's good, When you hooking up with that fool? She says, he wanted to hook up tonight, but I told him I'd call him back, so all I have to do is call him. Papi! You lucky I got a lot of love for you, 'for real' or I wouldn't be doing this, because I'm not feeling that 'puta' at all. He thinks he's getting some ass, but I ain't trying to fuck him. So whatever you got in mind, do it before he tries to fuck me o.k. Omega says, call him; tell him you wanna go chill, because you're bored. My man's and em are going to be following y'all. Whatever hotel y'all go to, get him out of his clothes and get the door unlocked. Go to the bathroom and hit me with the room number and my boy's will take it from there o.k. You hear anything! Just stay in the bathroom and don't come out until they tell you it's clear. Try to go to the Red-dog hotel; they don't have any cameras o.k. Tell him you like that spot. He won't be concerned with it; he just wants' to fuck o.k. You got dat. She says, "yeah papi" I got it. He kisses her on the forehead and leaves. Omega jumps in his car and rides to the back and picks up Ma'lik. Ma'lik says, what's up homey? Omega says, we have to squat for a minute. Therefore, they go back to the apartment where Rob's homie is. After about 2 hours, Karma calls Omega cell phone. She says, Omega! I'm not at a hotel, this fool brought me to his house, and he is high as hell and drunk. He's trying to show off, got his safe open, counting all his money, trying to impress me. If you're coming, come now. He lives in Teaneck, 131 McBride St; off Main Ave. I'm a try to keep him occupied o.k. I'm hiding in the bathroom now, but hurry up. Omega says, I-Iight then they hang up. Omega tells his angels of death what they have to do. He also tells Ma'lik, it might be some guap there for them, so go in, handle that, and get out. Don't waste time; and bring Karma back with them. Wipe the place clean of fingerprints too. Ma'lik says, I got it, and they ride out. **"The Angels of Death"** to claim yet another victim. They get to the house; it's a big pretty house. They hear dogs barking, but they are locked up in the fence, off to the side of the big house. They check the back door, its open. They case the joint. They see no one on the first floor, so they go upstairs. Upstairs, they see Karma and K'mar on the bed naked. Karma spots them, but K'mar is too out of it to notice. Karma tries to slip out of the bed, but K'mar grabs for her sluggishly. She says I'll be right back Papi, I'm going to the bathroom; He lies back down. When she gets into the bathroom, the 2 angels of death creep up on K'mar. By the time he notices them and goes for his gun, it's too late. Both barrels with silencers have already launched their hollow point bullets; and reached their mark. K'mar gasps for air. Ma'lik puts his hand over K'mar's mouth and says, 'shhh' breathe easy, let it go, its less painful. K'mar does and then… 'He's gone'. Ma'lik gets Karma out of the bathroom and say's get dressed. Then he looks around and say's Where the guap at? She says, move the dresser, he does. It's a safe; the door is open and its full of money and jewelry. He grabs one of the pillows, and takes the pillowcase off and fills it up with the money and jewels. All the time Ma'lik was doing this; Rob's homie was wiping down the knobs and furniture for prints. Ma'lik says, I-light, let's go; and they leave. In the car, Ma'lik calls Omega. He says, everything is green. Omega says, good; they hang up. When they get back to the apartment, they count the money. It was three hundred and fifty thousand cash, and over a hundred thousand in jewelry. Omega says, give homeboy the jewels and $100 grand and y'all take $125 grand apiece. Since he had come from long distance, they agreed; and he was very happy with his cut. Omega says, besides, he can get rid of it easier where he at, ain't that right homeboy. He says, "no doubt" with a smile. Omega says o.k. You ready to take off. He says, yeah! I'm out; gives Omega and J-Gun some dap and gives Karma a hug. Omega says; tell Tic and Rob I'll holla at them soon. He says I-light then. Then he jumps in his car and heads back to Washington like a thief in the night. Omega's cell phone rings, its Laura. She say's are you coming back here? He says I'm on my way now. She says o.k. See you when you get here; and they hang up.

He say's to Ma'lik drop Karma off for me. She says I wanted you to come home with me Papi. He says I can't tonight; I still have to take care of some business. She says will I see you tomorrow? He says yeah, I'll call you. She says o.k. Then they head out the door. In the car, Omega thinks about how smooth everything went; and hopes that they didn't forget to cover everything, so far, nothing went wrong. He goes over his plan and can't think of any errors he may have made. He's pleased with the way things went and he smiles to himself, because one of his problems has been eliminated. He got ninety-nine problems, but a bitch nigga named K'mar ain't one.....Anymore!

END OF CHAPTER XXXIII

CHAPTER XXXIV

"SHOOK ONE'S"

It's Monday, and it's back to business as usual. It's been a long weekend; no drugs were sold, so no money was made. The Narcs raided, but they only got a few fiends that were getting high in the abandoned apartments, however, there were no major arrests. Omega and J-Gun are standing out front of building 4. All of a sudden, an all black suburban truck drives thru; it stops right in front of building 4. J-Gun says, 'who the fuck is this.' Omega gestures to him stand fast homey, that looks like a Fed truck. J-Gun calms down. They can't see inside the truck, because of the jet-black, limo tinted windows. However, Omega's gut is telling him that they are 'police'. The truck stays in the middle of the street for about 15 minutes, then drives off. J-Gun says, what's that about? Omega says they are trying to intimidate people. Deep inside Omega, it was working, because he was starting to feel shook. He truly didn't want to end up like his father, Big Dixie. So he really started thinking hard about changing his lifestyle. He snaps out of the daze he was in, because he sees VS. He calls him over and says, what's good homey? VS. Say, what's good Mega. Omega says

I got a proposition for you. VS. Says, I-Iight, what's up? He says; let's take your talent to another level. I'm gonna start a label and I want you to be my star artist on it. VS. Say, that's what's up, I'm feeling that Mega, but I gotta eat. I got a Baby home dawg. Omega says, don't worry, we're gonna work something out, so you don't have to be on the block no more. But you gotta go in this studio and lay down your hottest shit, feel me! VS. Say, oh' no doubt. I'm a spitfire and let the people see what's really good, cause I'm the best thing smoking since the cigarette. And I'm a gonna spread like a incurable epidemic. Omega says I-Iight! That's what's up, that's what I want to hear. So this is what I'm gonna do, let me get this label thing right, then I'm a holla at you about the details I-Iight! VS. Say, I-Iight. Omega says, stay out of trouble doggie. He says, I'm gonna try real hard. Omega say's just give me a few days. They give each other some dap and say, 'one'. VS. Leaves and goes back to making his guap. Omega then turns to J-Gun and says, man! Shit is getting too thick for me, I' got to try and get some legit shit poppin' off. J-Gun says, I hear you. I was speaking to Precious a few days ago; and I'm gonna go and cop this building down there by her. It's a fifty-occupancy building. I'm gonna renovate it and rent it out. Plus I can see her more, I'm feeling her, she might be the one. Omega says word! For real! J-Gun smiles and says, true story, its going down like that. Omega says, that's good, I'm happy for you dawg, that's good news. Then Omega's cell phone rings, hello? It's Treecy. She says, big brah, have you seen Monty? He didn't come home last night. He says, no. She says, are you in the projects? He says, yeah. She says he might be up there somewhere. Please! Find him and make sure he is alright. He says, alright, I will. She says, o.k. Omega says, what ya doing? She says I'm chillin' with a few of my girlfriends from school. We are chatting on the computer, you know, doing girl stuff. He says, I-Iight, have fun and I'll find your brother o.k. She says o.k. I'll call you later, bye. Treeba, Zee, and Vita walk up. They say, hey! Mega, hey! 'J' and give them hugs.

Zee says have y'all heard that they found K'mar dead in his house. They are both emotionless and say, o'well, it was bound to happen. Somebody was gonna kill him sooner or later, the way he was wildin' out. Treeba say's the nigga is where he belongs. He starts too much shit. Now we have to worry about them bitches over there. I can't wait to see that bitch! Sheeka, I'm a kill her ass. Omega says, calm down cowgirl. You don't want to bring heat to yourself. The pigs are already on y'all for that shit that happened to Mira, so be easy, 'ya heard'. Then a car pulls up. A loud voice shouts out, HEY BITCHES! They see who it is and the girls scream, it's Carla. She had moved to Georgia for awhile to pursuit a modeling career; and was back to visit. She was also up this way, because she had a photo shoot in New York with a well-known fashion designer. She was hot! She was tall, slim, and very gorgeous. She showed the girls a recent photo she had took; and they said they had seen her in several magazines. They were worried that she had forgotten about them. However, Carla was hood. She just loved money, she was very independent, she was outspoken, and she wanted celebrity. However, she would never forget her home girls. They talked for a while, then Carla says, y'all want to come to this party with me? They all say hell yeah! Where it at? She says, in New York at the Cheetah club. All the new super models are going to be there, as well as the up and coming models. She says, its tonight, we'll leave out about 11:0clock, so be ready. They say that's what's up. Carla then says, I have to run off and go get a few things, but I'll see y'all tonight. So she jumps in her car and says bye and drive off. Omega says, Damn!! Carla is looking good and she's making it happen. She is what's really good. I'm proud of her, she gonna make it big someday. J-Gun says, yeah! She got it poppin' off right now. Omega says to J-Gun, yo' is that Monty walking in that building? He looks and says, it looks like him. Omega says, call him. J-Gun says, yo' Monty! Monty looks and waves. Omega says, yo' come here for a minute; Monty does. He says, what's up Mega? Omega pulls him to the side and says, where you been? Me and you're sister was worried about you. He says I'm good big brah; I can take care of myself. Omega says, I know that, but let somebody know when you're leaving, or when you're gonna stay Out. I'm not trying to be hard on you or nothing; I just want to make sure that you I-light o.k. You're my responsibility now. I promised our ol' man that I'd take care of you and Treecy, so give me that much I-light! Monty says, you got dat big brah, I'm sorry. I'm just so use to doing things on my own, I'll be more mindful o.k. Omega says, that's what's up. Omega says, you good? You need some doe? He says, no' I'm good. I'm a need a ride home in a minute though. Omega says, let me know when you're ready and I'll take you. Monty says o.k.

"AFTER AWHILE'

Omega pulls up in front of his house in Englewood and drops Monty off. As Monty is entering the door, Treecy calls out, "Monty is that you?" He says, yeah. She says, come in here for a minute. When he enters the entertainment room, Treecy says, I want you to meet my girlfriend 'Na-Na'. She wave and says, my name is Na'metria, but you can call me 'Na-Na' all of my friends do. Monty says, what's up. "Now Na'metria is 16. She a very pretty girl, long, silky hair, light skinned, very nice, hour glassed shape. However, she was HIV positive like Monty, but she took her medicine as directed from the Doctor. So she was maintaining her health as best, as she possibly can. She was born HIV positive from her mother." Monty says, o.k. Nice meeting you, Treecy I'll be in my room; and he goes to his bedroom. After a few minutes, Na-Na knocks on his door. Monty! May I come in? He says, yeah. When she enters, she says, WOW! You have a nice room. I see you like Pac, Biggie, and Huey P Newton. What you know about the Black Panthers? He says, I know a little, and I'm still learning. I read a lot on them. I get info off the computer. She says, that's what's up, educate yourself on your history. She says, why don't I see any pictures of your girlfriend? He says, I don't have one. She says, why not, a handsome guy like you. I know they be chasing you. He says nah' I'm good; I haven't been looking for one. She says, I don't have a boyfriend, so… can we be friends? He says, I guess we can be friends. She says so as friends, can we go to the movies this weekend, I would like to go see this real good movie that's playing. He says o.k. She says o.k. With a big smile. She says, I better get back in there with Treecy, but I'll talk to you later, is it o.k. If I call you? He says, yeah, o.k. She smiles, and then she walks back to the room where Treecy is. Once she gets back in the room, Treecy says, how did it go? She says, I think he likes me; we are going to the movies this weekend. Treecy says I hope he does too, then maybe he'll stay away from them projects. I love my brother, so I don't want him to be consumed by the stuff that goes on up there. I lost too many people I love up there, so I refuse to lose him.

END OF CHAPTER XXXIV

CHAPTER XXXV

"IT'S GOING DOWN"

Rob and Tic have the Boulevard on smash, every since Omega and J-Gun brought them home, gave them structure, and showed them how to bang for all the right reasons. Business has been beautiful. They are making a killin' off the drug game, getting that guap, makin that skrilla, Flipping work twice a week. Nothing light, all heavy shit. Omega and J-Gun have been networking with Laura and things are beautiful there with her too. They are making big profits with her, off her advice on the market. Omega knows he's being watched, so he's still a little shook. He started a record label called 'Aggress Records' and contracted VS. To be the first artist out on it. He also signed several other artists from the hood. A rap artist by the name of N-Ocent, and 2 R&B artists, Candy and Thug Casanova. The company is up and running and Omega landed a distribution deal with a major distributor. He had hot!!! Artists and everything was all good for the moment...

Omega is at the gas station on Market St getting gas; suddenly 3 black on black suburban trucks pull up and block him in. They make him get out of his car and put him in one of the trucks. And as several agents check his car, an agent that goes by the name of agent 'Floydio' interrogates him. He says, "Omega Styles." What's up scumbag? What you got in the car? Omega says, what you talking bout, I'm clean. Agent Floydio says, sure you are big balla, I know about you. I know what you do, and it's just a matter of time before I get your sleaze bag ass; and when I do, you're going away for a very, very, long time. Another agent comes back to the truck and says the car is clean. Agent Floydio says today is your lucky day douche bag, but you'll slip up, you guys always do. Now get the fuck out of my truck. Omega gets out of the truck and stands there while they pull off. He then goes to his car, heart pumpin' a hundred miles an hour, because he thought he was gone for sure. Usually when the Feds come and get you, they have something heavy on you already. Obviously they had nothing on him or he'd be on his way downtown right now. So he made up his mind, He was going to walk away. However, he made his bed, now he was going to have to lay in it, so walking away wasn't going to be that easy...

As he leaves the gas station, his cell phone rings, its Laura. She says, hey baby! What's up? He says, hey lovely, what's going on? She says, nothing much, just working hard and thinking of you. I wish I could be there with you right now, I'm so tense. I need a good massage and a good working over and nobody can do it but you. He say, is that right. She says, that is so right; and she laughs a little. Then she says, Omega I have something to tell you. He says, what's up? She says, umm, I umm. He says; don't be "scuurrred" spit it out, saying it jokingly. She say, I want you to know that I don't want to be a burden on you and you don't have to give me anything, because I'm alright financially. He says Laura, what are you talking about? Just say it. She says o.k. I'm pregnant, and I want to keep it.

There's silence for a while. She says, Omega! You there? He says, yeah, I'm here. He says, Laura I don't want to make it seem like I think you're a hoe or anything, but are you sure its mine? She says I'm positive Omega; I haven't been intimate with anyone else in about 18 months. He says how far are you? She says, 8 weeks. That's was the last time we were together; and that's what the Doctor told me. I wasn't sure, so I went to see her. She says, Omega! I said I wanted to keep it, not I am going to keep it. I wanted to speak to you about it first, to see how you felt about it. If you do not feel good about situation, I will go back to the Doctor and handle it. It's just that...I really wanted to have a baby and this is the first time I've ever been pregnant. Omega thinks for a minute and says, Laura! Have the baby; I don't know what I'm thinking about. I should be happy, because I don't have any kids, it'll be my first one too. She says happily, really Omega! He says, yeah! Have the baby. She says, I promise, I won't be a problem; and I will not expect us to be together. You can still have your freedom to do whatever it is you want to do. He says, I will be in the baby's life, so don't worry about anything, I'll take care of mine o.k. She says, o.k. whatever you want baby. She says, are you alright, how is business with Tic and Rob? He says, its lovely, but I'm done with it. I just went through some bullshit that I didn't like, so it's a wrap. I'll tell you about it when I see you face-to-face o.k. She says o.k. When am I going to see you? He says, real soon, I need to get away for awhile. Omega looks in his mirror, and he noticed that a car has been following him for awhile. He says, Laura I'll call you back a little later o.k. She says, alright; and they hang up. Now Omega always evade cars, because he doesn't like people to know where he live at. Therefore, he speeds up a little. The car speeds up with him. He makes a left. The car makes a left. He makes another left; the car turns with him again. He goes into a complete circle around the block and the car is still with him. So he says, to himself, alright muthafucka, let's see what you got. All of a sudden, Niggas pull out guns. It's K'mar's homies coming to avenge his death. They are hanging out the sunroof, windows, and all, shooting recklessly. One yells out,

"Time to die muthafucka." Omega pulls the Desert Eagle out of the stash spot that he has in the car. Bullets are wettin' up his car like lead rain. He's blazing bullets back at them and driving like his name was Jeff Gordon. A few of his bullets reach their target, bussin' the windows of the car chasing him. The dudes still blazin' bullets at him hit him a few times. He feels like he's on fire. He's wet and feeling weak, but continues to fire back. He fires off a few more rounds of bullets. The driver of the car is hit in the head, the car swerves side to side, and then crashes into some parked cars; bodies fly from the car. Omega sees the crash in his rear view, but he keeps it moving. He drives for awhile, then he pulls up is the pound and Big Sex and Shim-Shawn see the car shot up and run to it. They see Omega shot up and bleeding heavy. They yell, what happen dawg! What's up? Omega says niggas' tried to flat line me. Shim runs to the other side and pull him over. Big Sex jumps in and drives him to the hospital. Shim is like, hold on dawg we got you! You gonna be alright. We almost at the hospital. Omega doesn't know what's going on because he's semi-conscious. He has about 5 bullet holes in him and he's losing mad blood... He falls out. Back at the scene of the car crash, **"The Angel of Death"** claims yet some more souls...

"THE NEXT DAY"

Omega is laid up in the Hospital. He finally wakes up, and sees that he has mad patches on him; one covering every bullet hole that he has. He's in a lot pain, but he's alive. He's receiving a lot of flowers and balloons from family and friends. J-Gun walks in. He says, 'yo' what's good, how you feeling? I brought you something to eat. I know you ain't fucking with this bland ass Hospital food. Omega sits up to eat. J-Gun says, Laura called. I told her what happened; she said she's on her way up here. She was worried, because you didn't call her back last night. Oh' the dudes in the car that was chasing you, 3 are dead and 1 survived, but he's fucked up real bad from the crash. Omega says, 'J' that's it, I'm done. I can't handle this shit no more. I'm tired of watching over my shoulder, niggas trying to push me, Feds on my ass, it's a doney for me. I got to take care of Treecy, Monty, and my baby. J-Gun says, baby! What baby? You got a baby and I don't know about it dawg? Omega says, I just found out about it myself. Laura is pregnant. J-Gun says, damn! No wonder she was hysterical and speeding on the phone to get up here. Omega says, where's Treecy and Monty? J-Gun says, they were up here, but you were still knocked out, so they stayed awhile and I took them back home. I'll bring them back up tomorrow. The Doctor says you're going to be here a few weeks, at least 2. They still have to get a bullet out of you, because if it travels, you're in trouble. They said you can't do too much moving around, that will make it move, so be easy. Omega says, 'J' I'm leaving everything else to you. I'm taking what I got and I'm a just run the record label; and continue the shit with Laura. J-Gun says, Mega its over for me too. I'm a go to D.C. with Precious and do this real Estate thing. I'm a come back and forth, because of my property here and plus baby sis got accepted to a collage down the way. And I want to be your baby's Godfather. Omega says, yeah, that's what's up, that's good looking my dude. I guess we'll leave it to Big Sex and Sweets, they'll be glad to take it over, they know how to get that guap. J-Gun says that's what it is then. Listen, visits are almost over, so I'm a let you get some sleep, but I'll be back tomorrow with Treecy and Monty I-light. Omega says, I-light, E.S. J-Gun says, all the time; and he leaves...

About a week and a half later' Omega is getting dressed; the Doctor says he is well enough to go home today. A nurse walks in, she says, are you ready to go? You're friend is down stairs waiting on you. Omega starts to walk out the door. She says, no honey, I have to take you down in the wheel chair. He says I can walk; I'm strong enough now. She says, maybe so, but I have to, its procedure. He looks at her and says, alright, I don't want to get you in trouble; you have been nice to me. Therefore he sits down and she pushes him to the front entrance in the wheel chair. As he gets out the chair, he says, here, this is for you; and he tries to hand her an envelope. She says, aah, aah, it's my job to do what I do. He says, I know, but it's just a thank you card. She says, oh' how nice, thank you. He says, you're very welcome, thank you for looking after me; and nice meeting you; he gives her a hug, jumps in the car and they pull off. The nurse opens the card and she has 10 one hundred-dollar bills inside with a nice thank you card. She looks up at the car as they drive down the street and she smiles to herself.

Inside the car' J-Gun is hesitant on telling Omega what's going on, but he has to. He says, Omega! We have a problem. Omega looks at him concerned, what's good dawg. What's going on? J-Gun says, Monty was kidnapped. Omega blacks out. What the! Who the fuck! Who got em, did you hear from anybody? J-Gun says, Yeah! Some muthafucka keeps calling your house, talking bout they want 500 grand cash or they'll kill him. Omega says, how long has he been missing? J-Gun says, since yesterday. Omega says dawg! You should have been told me this shit. J-Gun says, Omega you wasn't in no condition to do anything, you're still kinda fucked up. I was going to take care of the shit myself, but they haven't called back yet. Omega says, damn!! Good-looking dawg, my bad. Damn!!! It seems like every time a muthafucka tries to get out the game, something pulls his ass right back in, this is the bullshit. J-Gun says I got the money in the trunk. Omega says, good look dawg, but I got it in the house. Then Omega gets a call on his cell. The caller ID says 'private caller' Omega usually doesn't answer blocked calls, but since Monty is missing, he's answering every call. He says, hello! The voice says, is this Omega? He says, yeah, who dis? The voice says, don't worry about that, all you need to know is that, "an enemy, of your enemy, is your friend" Now! Do you want to get Monty back? Omega says, yeah, what do you want? The voice says, I know you're kidnappers are asking for 5 hundred large, get me 3 hundred and I'll tell you where you can find him. What you do after that is on you. Omega says where should I bring the money? The voice says; bring it to Eastside Park tonight at 12:00 clock sharp. Once I have the money, I'll tell you where you can find the info. Omega says, how do I know I can trust you? The voice says, you can't, but if you want him back, you will. Omega says, I-Iight, I'll be there. The voice says, tonight and hangs up. J-Gun says, was that them? He says, no, it was somebody else talking bout they know how to get him back. J-Gun looks at him with a confused look. Omega says, go to the pound for a minute; J-Gun does. Omega sees Ma'lik. He says, Ma'lik! Jump in; I need to talk to you for a minute. Ma'lik says, what's good my dude; then he jumps in the car. He says, what's up dawg? Omega says, somebody kidnapped Monty and I need you to help me get him back. Ma'lik gets upset, he says, who got em, I'll kill the muthafucka. Omega says, we don't know, we'll find out tonight, hopefully. He says, let me know, I'll handle that shit for you on the love, feel me. Omega says that's what's up; I'll let you know what's good tonight. Ma'lik starts to get out of the car. He says, Omega! Make sure. You know that's my thing, I got you on that, that's my word. Omega says I-Iight, E.S. Ma'lik say, all the time. He then turns to J-Gun and say; take me home, so I can check on Treecy. I know she is sick out of her mind right now. So J-Gun jumps on the highway. After awhile' they pull up in front of Omega's house, the dogs greet him waging their tales like crazy, because they haven't seen their master in a few weeks. Omega opens the door and yells out Tre! You here? She says, yeah! I'm in my room. He walks upstairs to her room and she's in there with Na-Na, they are looking sad and down. She says, Omega what are we gonna do? He hugs her and says, don't worry, we'll get him back, I promise, he'll be alright. He looks at them and they both have tears in their eyes. He says I'm working on getting him back now. He asks J-Gun, what time is it? J-Gun says, 8:00 Clock. He says, we still have a little time, Tre did they call again? She says, yeah, earlier, but they said they wanted to speak to you. I told them you'd be here later, so maybe they'll call back. He says o.k. We'll wait on the call. About 3 hours later' the telephone rings, Omega picks it up, hello! It's a woman's voice, she says, Omega there yet? Omega says this me. She says, hey muthafucka! If you want this fag back, get me that money by 3:00am and be ready to drop it off, If not, you'll find him floatin' in the river with some hot shit in em by 6. Omega says, you don't have to do that, I'll have the money, just tell me where to bring it. The woman's voice says, I'll call back at 2, to tell you where to bring it; and if I get any, and I mean any, funny shit, the punk is dead; and hangs up. Omega hangs up and says, damn! Back at Vita's apartment,' Ma'lik is getting ready to put in work. Vita says, where you going? Ma'lik says I got to go take care of something important. She says what? He says, I can't tell you. She says I hope you ain't going nowhere to get into trouble. He says I got to go handle this. She says, no Ma'lik, don't go, stay here with me. He says, I can't 'V' I got to handle this. (They argue back and forth for awhile) Then he says, look don't say, anything, promise you won't. She says, I promise. He says, Monty was kidnapped and I got to go help Omega get him back o.k. You satisfied. She looks at him concerned, there's nothing she could really say, but Ma'lik please be careful. He says, I will. I'll be back, don't worry o.k. He grabs both of his guns, give her a kiss and walks out the door. She looks out the window and sees him standing there waiting on Omega. She runs to the room, puts on all black, grabs her ratchet with the silencer, runs back to the window, and waits for Omega to pull up. She sees 2 cars driving up from down the street, one is Omega's car, the other is Sweet's car, and so she runs out the door. They pull off; she jumps in her car and follows them. They drive to Eastside Park. She watching from afar, she sees J-Gun get out the car and sit a duffel bag by the stairs of the little castle in the Park. He jumps back in the car, they drive up a little and J-Gun jumps back out, digs in a garbage can and pulls out a yellow envelope, then they drive off again, leaving the Park. As she pulls out of the hiding spot, watching everything, she sees someone appear out of the darkness and grab the duffel bag off the stairs; however, she can't see the face. She follows them for awhile, keeping a safe distance not to be noticed. They wound up in Passaic, and the cars start to park. 'In Omega's car' Omega got the envelope with the address and info to where Monty is being held. He says, look, the house is down the street, everybody knows what to do, whoever gets Monty, hit me on the bleep and be out. Be careful and be on point, I-Iight, its **"Bang Boy or Die Boy,"** so let's ride; and they start to get out the car. 'Back in Vita's car' she sees Omega, J-Gun, Ma'lik, Big Sex, and Sweets exit the cars, so she gets out and follows in the shadows, quietly. They come up to a condemned looking house; they split up and go in. Vita goes around the back and notices some movement through a basement window; she sees Monty tied up in a chair looking a little worried. She also sees Sheeka and some other girl she doesn't know. All of a sudden she hears gunfire, Sheeka says, watch him and runs out to see what's going on. Vita thinks quick, now is her chance to move. She opens the window a little and hits the girl with 3 hot shots of silent death, and quickly climbs in. She looks at Monty and says, 'shhh', so he does. She hides behind the door and waits for Sheeka to come back in the room. On the other side of that door' niggas are bangin' out, putting in mad work, it sounds like Vietnam. Sheeka runs back in the room with her gun out, and she sees the girl lying on the floor dead. So like in slow motion, she turns around to Monty pointing the gun at him and as she squeezes the trigger, she is hit up 3 times by **"Death with an Angels face"** but not before she gets a shot off. **BLOW!!!** She hits Monty in the chest with a single shot, and falls to the floor. Omega, Ma'lik, and J-Gun run in the room and they are shocked at what they see. They see Vita untying Monty crying. They see the dead bodies on the floor and notices one of them is Sheeka. Ma'lik says, Vita! What the fuck you doing here? She says crying, I followed y'all, to help get Monty back. He's shot we got to get him to a Hospital, hurry up! Grab him! They grab Monty and head for the door. They meet up with Sweets and Big Sex. They have gunshot wounds, but nothing life threatening. They all jump in the cars and speed off. As they are leaving, they hear police car sirens blazing to where they were at. They avoid being seen by the police and get Monty to the Hospital. Back at the condemned house' **"The Angel of Death"** claims yet more souls, However, One soul he doesn't claim; and the body is still breathing, regardless to how many bullets it took, its still breathing. The cops arrive on the scene and tape off the whole block.

"A FEW WEEKS LATER"

In Omega's house' Omega walks up the stairs and into Monty's room. He looks around the room and he's sad, because he's imagining the room without Monty, but then he looks over to the bed and sees Treecy, Na-Na, and Monty smiling and playing. Monty is bandaged up; fortunately he was only hit with a flesh wound, in between his chest and arm. He kisses Monty on the forehead, then kisses Treecy and says I'll be back; I have to go take care of something real quick. Call me on my cell if y'all need me. The dogs are out, so y'all should be o.k. alright, I'll be back; then he walks out the door. He jumps in his car, then makes a call to his record label, the receptionist answers; she recognizes the voice and says, hey! Mr. Styles, how are you? He says much better thank you. How are things there? She says, very good, its business as usual. He says, good, I'll be there shortly. She says o.k. See you then; they hang up. As he pulls up in the pound, he sees the Feds putting Ma'lik in a car. He parks, then he sees Sweets, he calls him over. He asks, what happened? Sweets say, they took Vita downtown for questioning; now they're taking Ma'lik. They have been up here all day asking questions. J-Gun pulls up, He says, what's going on? Omega says, I don't know, but we'll find out. Omega says, oh' Sweets me and J-Gun decided that we're turning the business over to you and Big Sex, we're done, we have some other things we need to be doing ya' heard. Then Omega gets on his cell and calls his lawyer. He tells him to go downtown and find out what the charges are on Vita and Ma'lik, the Lawyer gets right on his job. About an hour later' he calls Omega back and says, they were questioning both of them about the murders that happened in Passaic. They were supposedly seen at the Scene of the crime. You're friend Vita was identified, so their holding her, also Ma'lik was identified and his record is extensive for gun charges, so they are holding him for further questioning. They have not set a bail, so they are going to have to sit for awhile. Omega says, I'm a need you to represent them, so do what you have to and I'll be there to see you on the fee. The Lawyer says o.k. Omega says, thank you Mr. McCall. He says, no problem; and they hang up. J-Gun says, what's up with them? Omega tells him what the Lawyer said. J-Gun says, I hope Vita doesn't roll over, you know how persuasive those dirty ass cops are. Omega says, she won't, she's a soldier, she'll ride or die.

"MONTHS LATER"

Several months later in trial' Omega and the whole crew are sitting up in court. The Prosecutor is about to bring in his star witness, it's Sheeka. People are shocked because everybody thought she was dead. The Prosecutor puts her on the stand and starts to examine her. She tells the whole story of what happened; however, when the Prosecutor asks her, do she see the shooters in court today? She says, no. The Prosecutor is confused, he says, you don't see the shooters here of the night in question? She says "no" I do not. Now Sheeka thought about it a while why she was lying up in the bed in the Hospital. At first, she wanted the police to send them to jail, but then she realized that she wouldn't get any gratification out of that. She wanted to see them suffer. Therefore, she wanted them where she can get to them easily... on the street, so she could get revenge. The Prosecutor asked her again. She confidently said it was not them. The Prosecutor said you identified them as the shooters when you were at the Hospital. She said I was under a lot of medication, therefore I wasn't in my right state of mind, but now that I see them I am 100% sure that it was not them. The Judge calls both counselors to the podium, they say a few words then he dismisses the jury for a short break and has a meeting with the Lawyer and Prosecutor in his chambers. About an hour later' they come back out, the Judge sends for the jury. I thank you fine people of the jury for your participation in the trial proceedings, however this matter has been resolved, so you are all dismissed. Then he announces, "due to insufficient evidence and mistaken identity, the charges are being dropped against Vita and Ma'lik. However, due to Ma'lik's arrest, he has violated his parole obligations and must finish out the remainder of his sentence in jail which is 18 months". (This was just a way to keep Ma'lik off the streets for a little while; they couldn't get him on the shootings, so a parole violation was the next best thing.) Vita was set free, she shouts to Ma'lik, I'm a wait for you and I'm gonna hold you down. Ma'lik looks at her and winks his eye, he says, its nothing, I'll be home in a minute. Omega says we got you homeboy, just holla when you need somethin' 'ya' heard.' Ma'lik looks at him and nods his head and says, 'I heard.' Omega looks at the State Prosecutor and can tell that he is furious, because his whole case went straight out the window. Omega then looks at Sheeka and she has a look on her face that can kill. In Sheeka's mind, she's thinking, yeah! Muthafuckas enjoy this shit now, because when I get the fuck up out of this wheel chair, all of y'all are some dead Muthafuckas. Then she smiles to herself with a devilish grin; and was escorted back out of the courtroom by the nurse that brought her in.

"DAYS LATER"

A few days later' Omega is by J-Gun's house helping him finish getting ready to leave. He's going to Washington to live a normal life, his ripping and running days are over. However, he say's to Omega, if you ever need me dawg for anything, I'll be here you know that, I'm a **"Bang Boy, Die Boy" for life.** Omega says, 'I heard.' Then he says, you act like you're leaving forever, I know you're gonna come back and forth to see you're godson. J-Gun says I know that's right. He then yells, Ja'lyn! Let's go, time to roll. His sister says, here I come. She walks out the now empty house and hugs Omega and say, goodbye for now uncle Omega, tell Treecy and Monty that I love them and I'll keep in touch o.k. He says, o.k. Baby girl stay getting all A's in school. She says, I will, I promise. J-Gun hugs Omega and say, E.S. homeboy. Omega says, all the time. Then him and Ja'lyn jump in the truck and wave as they are driving off. Omega stands there with a smile and watch them pull out; and then he jumps in his car and takes out his cell phone and says, hey! Y'all alright, a voice says, yeah, we're o.k. He says o.k. I'm on my way home; and as he drives back to his house in Englewood, he thinks to himself, how lucky he is to be alive and have both Treecy and Monty with him, then he smiles. However, he doesn't know that Chaos and Mayhem remains to be seen in his near future...

To be Continued...

Acknowledgements and Thank U's

First and foremost I would like to thank **G.O.D.** because without him none of this would be possible. I would like to thank my beautiful wife Zina and our beautiful children, Lil' Devine, Akera, Naisa, and her lil' one teriona. (I'll ride and die for them, 'true story') I would like to acknowledge all of my family, I have a very big Family, so I'm going to name last names, however, if I don't name you, I still love you with all of my heart. Lewis's, McKnight's, McBride's, Drakefords, Keys, Allen's, Myles, Higgins, Aunt Jane & Warren and the Williams family, McDowell's, Cato's, Clyburne's, Roberson's, Dickerson, Special shout out to Aunt Gloria & Uncle Richard for all the love and support and being positive role models for me and my wife. Special shout out to Laurie, Jamar, and Allie Easton in Lakewood. My daughter La'tonda whom I love dearly. My godson Zaire, his mother Stacy, Lil' Antoine and Kenny. Special shout out to Reggie & Barbara thanks for being good friends. Special shout out to Tom Colandro for helping me out in the computer room. Special thanks to Mr. Mike Myers and Mr. K Kinch at Tully House for the advice and help. Special shout out to my dude, Mark 'Young Buck' Wells for all the support, you my dun, dun 4-life nigga. His wife and kids Tracy, Terrell, and Nelly. The Harvey family for their love and support. All of those ladies in my wife's card circle.

Special shout out to Missy & Bryant, Niecy & Bryant, Colleen & Pullet, Candice & Rashad, Kyron and his Lil' one, Gerrauo, Aunt Tootsie, My Aunt Leona and her family in Florida. Ta'nisha & Troy, Ebony, Shakira & Steve and her Lil' one. My sisters and their army of Lil' ones, Sabrina, Nute, Princess, Wowis. My brother J.J. and his Lil' Ones. My cousin Devon McKnight for holding me down when shit got thick, good lookin' big brah love you and your fam, jenn, London, All my brothers in the struggle and fight against oppression and destruction. All my niggas up in the Pound where I grew up at Big L, JT, Tap, Shim, B.D. Lord E, Moe, Big Rob, Rich, Mike g, Ski, Craig, Aboob, Rog A.K.A double R, Chink, Sha', yusef, Ra'von, Franchi, KeKe Yannie, KeKo, all my niggas up there. All My niggas I met while Incarcerated, especially the ones in Northern State. SK, Paco, Homicide, Gameface, JB, Shorts. My big homey Bloodshed love you big brah. My nigga Corey 'C' Armstead, My niggas Sha'doo, CL, Y-Kim, Tasha, Tanika,Jihad, Hafsan, Doug AKA Damier, Fifty, LB, Paul, Trav, Daymond aka N-Ocent, Cool Shoes, Dirt, Rob, Doc, Black, Mu and Blacksun from Talbot Hall. IB and Born Hall, Kiesha, Volanta, Lisa, Bobbie, Tramina, Michelle, Tonya. My brother-In-laws, Barry, Derrick, Anthony, and Floyd. All My wife's partners and all the people who went out to go buy the book and if I forgot to Mention You I'll get you in the next one. Also thanks to the following people, Renegade Foxxx, Bobby, Mike Cameron, Dennis, Ricky, Allen, Junior, Malik, Armando, Steve, Shaft, B.U., Mike Porter, Chuck, Chubb, Whimp, Tony, Peanut, Nook, Dwayne, Born, Born Black, Fa'heem, Great, and Dubar. **"I can do all things through Christ, which who strengthens me"** Power to the People, and God bless.

Joseph Lewis

A-K-A
Devine Mayhem

"THE CHARACTERS"

Males

Omega Styles, aka "Omega" -plays- kingpin drug dealer

Jaffar Gunthorpe, aka "J'Gun" -plays- Omega's right hand man

Sweets, -plays- pretty boy of Omega's crew (ladies man)

Ma'lik -plays- gun happy homeboy (Omega's homie)

Shim Shawn -plays- athlete turn drug dealer (hood legend)

Big Dixie -plays- drug kingpin that went to prison (father)

Big Sex -plays- big sexy thug nigga, but gets high (model type)

K'mar -plays- Other gang banger from out of town (Omega's nemesis)

Fury -plays- out of control thug (K'mar's homie)

Clipse -plays- K'mar's homie

Tic -plays- Washington D.C. drug dealer

Rob -plays- Washington D.C. drug dealer

VS: -plays- battle rapper that makes it out of the hood

Monty -plays- Sex abused Boy

Marvin Priest -plays- Chief of police

Devon Steele -plays- 'Black' police officer grew up in the hood (Narcotics)

Ben Stickler -plays- 'Black' corrupt police officer (Narcotics)

Jessy Grimes -plays- 'white' police officer that goes by the book (Narcotics)

Tonio Mendez -plays- 'Hispanic' police officer, grew up in the hood (Narcotics) 'fair'

Jake & Jack -plays- mysterious feds in truck

Females

Karma aka caliente -plays- high maintenance project chick

Vicki Steele -plays- drug attic mother

Treecy -plays- Sex abused girl

Vita -plays- little girl that gets shot when younger and becomes traumatic assassin when older

Zee -plays- very pretty innocent chick from projects

Carla -plays- zee's best friend

Treeba -plays- pretty thug chick, always 730

Mira -plays- nice project chick (K'mar's girl)

Sheeka -plays- Mira's best friend

Precious -plays- J'Gun's girl from Maryland

Laura -plays- Lady Stockbroker

Misa -plays- Big Dixie's mistress

Meagan Bunz -plays- 'Black' woman police officer, who grew up in the hood, got family in the hood

Printed in the United States
by Baker & Taylor Publisher Services